M000196356

No Flowers Required

Required

a Love Required novel

Cari Quinn

This book is a work of fiction. Names, characters, places, and incidents are the product of the author's imagination or are used fictitiously. Any resemblance to actual events, locales, or persons, living or dead, is coincidental.

Copyright © 2012 by Cari Quinn. All rights reserved, including the right to reproduce, distribute, or transmit in any form or by any means. For information regarding subsidiary rights, please contact the Publisher.

Entangled Publishing, LLC
2614 South Timberline Road
Suite 109
Fort Collins, CO 80525
Visit our website at www.entangledpublishing.com.

Brazen is an imprint of Entangled Publishing, LLC. For more information on our titles, visit www.brazenbooks.com.

Edited by Heather Howland
Cover design by Heather Howland

ISBN   978-1-62266-823-6

Manufactured in the United States of America

First Edition August 2012

The author acknowledges the copyrighted or trademarked status and trademark owners of the following wordmarks mentioned in this work of fiction: *Arachnophobia*; Coors; Tilt-A-Whirl; Beatles/White Album; Christian Louboutin; *Sports Illustrated*; *Popular Mechanics*; NYU; Wharton; *Dante's Inferno*; MacBook Air; Superman; PayPal; Nike; Windex; *The Big Bang Theory*; Twizzlers; *Family Guy*; Harley-Davidson; Silverado; Cirque du Soleil; Smurf; Rolling Stones; GQ.

To my biggest fan, my mom, even though I don't let her read my books. And to Taryn Elliott, who is the wind beneath my wings (even when they're clipped.)

Chapter One

This was officially the crappiest day of Alexa Conroy's life.

"Is there anything else I can do for you?" Harvey Walton, her real estate agent, asked. He'd called to make sure she was happy with how the sale of her home had gone, and she'd yet to do little more than answer in short sentences.

She'd sold her dream house for a very good price in a depressed market. How could she complain? The discount-store violet Harvey had sent didn't exactly thrill her, but she couldn't fault the gesture. Nope, it was the obvious red-and-white sticker of her nemesis, Value Hardware, on the bottom of the pot she faulted, not Harvey.

The only good thing about her new apartment was that she wouldn't have to see her nemesis down the block unless she pressed her forehead against the window. And since said window had enough grime to reduce the outward view significantly, she wasn't going to touch the thing, especially with her face.

"No, thanks," she said, setting the violet on the windowsill. Judging from its wilted state, it would probably be dead in a couple days. "Out of curiosity, why did you choose to buy the violet from Value Hardware? I assure you no one on their staff knows flowers like I do."

At Harvey's silence, she gusted out a sigh. She didn't need to take out her frustration on him. It wasn't his fault that if she saw one more of Value's signature smiley-face balloons around town she'd probably go postal. Or was it floral, since she operated a floral shop?

"I'm sorry, Harvey," she said, pressing her fingertips against her forehead. God, she needed a massage. Not in the budget, buttercup. "I appreciate all your help. You made the whole process painless." As painless as it could be to sell the house she'd hoped to live in for the rest of her life. But she'd done it for the right reasons, and that made all the difference. No doom and gloom here. "So I should receive the check by next week?"

"By the end of next week, definitely."

Her brain blinked out on his talk of administrative procedures as she noticed the large spider building a tapestry—screw calling it a web, this thing was big enough to occupy a wall of a museum—in the closet where she'd planned on putting her clothes. Her designer wardrobe just happened to be the last shred of her freewheeling, party-girl lifestyle. She didn't even get to have the sex that went with it anymore, since she'd involuntarily taken up celibacy as a participant sport.

Despite her general malaise lately, she wasn't going to balk about killing one of God's creatures out of misplaced sympathy. There was a line that couldn't be crossed by man or nature. Infringing on her woefully inadequate closet space was it.

"Alexa?" Harvey asked. "Are you still there?"

"Yeah, sorry. I have a situation to attend to. But thanks again, and I'll be sure to call the next time I have a real estate—" She broke off. Uh-uh. No. The only real estate she had left was her shop, and that was rented. She had no intention of looking for new retail space, so she would have no use for Harvey. Ever. "Take care, Harvey," she said with her brightest smile as she clicked off.

Time to do some bug excavation.

She sidestepped her marmalade cat, Trixie, who seemed intent on tripping her, and seized her damp sponge and bucket. The whole apartment needed a thorough scour before she settled in, if she even could. She certainly didn't have many comforts of home yet. Her flat-screen TV, long leather couch, Tiffany-style floor lamp, and two end tables, plus her queen-size air mattress and the battered kitchen table left from the previous tenants, filled most of the space.

Oh, and she couldn't forget the contents of her "bedroom." She winced at the curtain of purple beads she'd jerry-rigged to section off the alcove that contained her air mattress. All she needed was a lava lamp and a black light and she'd be in her own sixties nightmare.

Narrowing her eyes, she studied the spider and its spindly legs. Already she could feel her resolve wavering. She glanced at the windows. Maybe she could dump the spider on the fire escape.

She glanced at her fat sponge. Or she could smash it and move on with her day.

Pretend it's Value Hardware. That she could do.

All she had to do was visualize the hardware store's sterile white walls and its annoyingly efficient robot-slash-droid-slash-checkout people, who were only too happy to load discount flower displays into the backs of minivans. After all, they had half an aisle of hastily assembled arrangements. Why visit Alexa's store, Divine Flowers, when a person could make do with something that cost half as much?

Craftsmanship and exquisite blooms didn't mean much in a crappy economy, and she got that. Hell, her own personal economy was currently in the shitter, so how could she quibble?

She needed to off the happy little spider—which really wasn't that monstrous in the right light—and get cleaning the rest of her new dwellings.

Water. That would kill the spider more humanely. Right.

Determined, she marched into the bathroom to turn on the faucet, prepared to soak her sponge and kick spider ass. A gush of liquid fountained down her front. "Holy shit. Seriously?"

Grumbling, she knelt to study the pipes, sure she could figure this out on her own. Was a washer loose? Maybe if she dug her screwdriver out of her pink ladies' toolbox she could tighten something. Or screw something. Or *something* something to stop the damn water now trickling on the floor.

She'd been a homeowner and she ran a business, solo. Surely she could—

At the sound of water burbling in the pipes, she squealed and overcompensated, falling back on her butt. Over went the bucket and sponges she'd dropped the first time she'd gotten sprayed. Her ass hit the cracked tile floor hard, jarring her bones and bruising her in unpleasant places.

Before she could be treated to any more impromptu baths, she crawled up on her knees and turned off the spigot. The chlorine-scented water had already made the place reek like a pool house. She rubbed her damp forehead and caught her breath. Or tried to.

First she'd discovered that the air-conditioning was undependable at best, and it was only mid-August. Now this. What if this was just the beginning? If there were water issues, how would she wash her dishes? How would she bathe?

"Oh my God. Breathe." She rose and willed herself not to have a panic attack. She hadn't had one in years, and now would not be a good day to start.

Everything was fine. First day in her new place and she had an extra from Arachnophobia chilling in her closet and a nonfunctional sink. No big deal.

"You forgot that tonight you're sleeping on an air mattress shielded by a beaded curtain," she muttered at her reflection, taking in her lopsided topknot and the streak of dirt on her cheek. She'd also developed a few more wrinkles since this morning, which probably wasn't too surprising.

She smudged the lines on the mirror and noticed they came off on her fingertips. At this point, she almost preferred thinking her age-relief face cream had failed. Otherwise it meant she'd moved into a serious dump, and if so, whose fault was that?

The afternoon she'd signed the rental agreement—the day she'd put her gorgeous mountain hideaway on the market— came roaring back with sterling clarity. The only thing that had mattered was finding a cheap, affordable apartment close to work. Couldn't get much closer than two flights above her store, right? The rest of the building looked snazzy enough— on the outside. On the inside, it was a big ol' mess.

But she wasn't going to stand for it. She'd be damned if she dealt with face-eating spiders and bathroom flooding in the same day.

She refastened her sloppily chic bun. Her makeup had worn off hours ago and her cute purple top no longer looked so fresh. Especially not with the giant water splotch over one breast. Too bad she didn't have the time or energy to change. Besides, the odds were slim she'd encounter a hot guy on her way to speak to the scarily efficient-looking building manager.

Her long skirt clung to her legs, but it didn't alter her

single-minded march across her apartment. She had her game face on, and she was prepared to do battle. They wouldn't railroad her into accepting deplorable conditions. She'd just demand that her sink be serviced immediately. Then she'd do a quick tidying job on the apartment, clean herself up, and go have dinner with her best friend, Nellie.

She headed down the hall, only wobbling a bit on her waterlogged Christian Louboutins. The audible squish really didn't add anything to her mood, but she had more important things to worry about at the moment.

Abruptly, Alexa stopped in front of an open apartment door and widened her eyes. Who was *that?*

A man wearing tight jeans and a black T-shirt stretched tight over a taut back meant for fingernail marks knelt in the middle of an apartment with a floor plan just like hers, methodically ripping up strips of the laminate. He faced away from her, which gave her the perfect opportunity to study the bunch and flex of muscles in his sinewy forearms. He wore some sort of copper cuff around one wrist, and a tattoo flashed from under the sleeve on his other arm. She couldn't make out what the tat was, but one thing she could discern with no trouble at all.

Beefcake boy had a hell of an ass.

Which brought her thoughts around full circle to her streak of celibacy. She couldn't fix all the problems in her life in one go, but was a night of blow-the-roof-off spectacular sex too much to ask for?

No. It damn well wasn't. Besides, there was more to life than work, and she was doing everything she could there. She'd started to import more specialty flowers from far-flung places. Delicate blooms rarely seen around the hills of Pennsylvania. She'd hired an amazing new floral designer at substantial cost. Soon, no one would doubt that Divine Flowers was a force to be reckoned with. With her new designer, she would be more equipped to handle splashier events. Eventually, when the budget allowed, she'd be able to hire a whole *team* of designers.

Divine would survive. Thrive, even. No matter what it took.

She knocked on the open door, then knocked again when he kept working. Diligent. She liked that. "Excuse me?"

"Yeah?"

That he didn't turn to face her moderately grated, but hey, she still had his ass to observe. She didn't mind talking to his backsi—err, back.

Better yet, perhaps she'd found someone to make her very happy to be alive for a few hours. Someone who would make her forget about huge spiders, possibly ruined boots, and impending financial collapse. Maybe, just maybe, this guy would fit the bill.

Though she should probably talk to him before she started plotting sexcapades.

"I'm assuming you're the building handyman?" she prompted.

His lengthy hesitation earned him a frown he didn't bother to shift around to see. "Need some service, ma'am?"

Her frown spread. She wasn't used to being ignored, at least not when she'd almost made up her mind to rock his world. "I have a leak."

He set down his stripping tool and swiveled on his knees toward her. Though he wasn't smiling, he didn't seem annoyed by the interruption either. A handy thing, that, since his face sucked the thoughts from her head. *Yeah. He'll do.*

She was due a karmic windfall after all she'd gone through recently, wasn't she? Maybe this—*he*—was it.

If not, there was always the purple wand with butterfly

attachment in her suitcase.

She wouldn't have called him traditionally handsome. His jaw was too square, his eyebrows too slashing. A copper ring highlighted one of them, stealing her attention from his large, long-lashed eyes, though from this distance she couldn't tell their color. He wore his dark blond hair in a buzz cut, grown out enough to make her want to feel the prickle against her palm.

His mouth quirked when she continued to silently catalog his features as if he were the featured male model in an underwear advertisement. Slowly, he dragged his own gaze down her body, but she didn't look down to see what he saw. He held her riveted, as did that intriguing fluttering thing happening in her belly. She hadn't fluttered in regard to a man in way too long.

"You do look a little…wet." He didn't smile, but his amusement came through loud and clear.

Alexa looked down and gasped. Her flowing cream skirt with its miniature purple flowers had gone from sheer to transparent. It stuck to her legs from ankle to hip, highlighting everything—including her blush-pink panties. She might as well have not been wearing a slip at all.

"It's the sink," she managed, so mortified that her throat closed around the words. She could deal with moving out of her dream home. Could handle extreme business competition. What she couldn't face were fashion faux pas that led to entertaining random handymen. "I was going to clean and the sink threw up all over me!"

"*You* were cleaning, princess?" He rose from the floor and rubbed his forearm over the sweat beading on his forehead. No wonder. This apartment was like an oven set on broil.

Her store had functional AC, something that was necessary for her flowers. She'd been told the units all had air-conditioning as well, but apparently that didn't apply to this one.

She crossed her arms over her chest and thanked God her damp top was royal purple and therefore not see-through. "Who are you calling princess? And how do you know what I clean or don't clean, plumber?"

"Who said I intended to help you with your plumbing problem?" He bent to pick up his toolbox and strode to the doorway, taking a moment to tower over her when she refused to give way. She didn't doubt the move was intentional. "And didn't anyone ever teach you it's not nice to make fun of the help?"

He had to be six inches taller than her, at a minimum. Considering she was five-eight, she didn't meet a lot of guys who could tower over her. Or even lean much. When combined with the raw, sexual pheromones he exuded along with the faint, clean scent of perspiration, she couldn't quite breathe properly. The chlorine fumes must've screwed with her lung function.

"You called me princess. Plumber is hardly an insult, if that's one of your job responsibilities," she said, stepping aside. If she didn't, he'd probably call her more names and drip sweat on her. Actually he'd probably produce more just to prove he wasn't lacking in the testosterone department. He seemed like the type.

Again he swept his gaze up and down her body, but not in a sexual manner. More like he was appraising her as he might a particularly thick slab of drywall. "You wear the clothes of one, you get the title. So about that leak of yours…"

"In my apartment." She balled her hands into fists. "My bathroom sink."

"Ah. Glad you clarified." He walked ahead of her down the hall, pushing open the door of number 33 without waiting for her direction. "You know, this doesn't really strike me as your sort of place. How did a woman like you end up here? Though I've gotta say, nice furniture. Leather and Tiffany." He winked at her over his gigundo shoulder. "Princess."

She fought not to sniff. "There's nothing wrong with this building." It was one thing for her to think negative thoughts about her new home. *He* wasn't allowed. "And how did you know which apartment was mine?"

Was he some sort of peeper? Had he crept along the fire escape outside her apartment and watched her blow up her air mattress? Maybe he knew her from her shop. People came in and out all the time. Not enough people, but still.

He didn't respond, just set down his toolbox in the bathroom with a clatter. Without comment, he went to the kitchen and did something under *that* sink before reappearing in the bathroom doorway. "What seems to be the problem?"

How many times did she need to say the same thing? She pointed to the bathroom sink. "The sink leaks. *This* sink, not the kitchen one."

"Got that. I had to turn off the main water valve or else you're going to get wet all over again." He stole another quick glance at her damp skirt, probably figuring she wouldn't notice.

Oh, she noticed, all right.

She startled as Trixie—the only cat in the history of cats who actually liked water—emerged from behind the shower curtain and hightailed it into the kitchen. "Whatever. For the final time, I turned on *this* sink to get some water for my bucket—the water smells, by the way—and it shot out all over me."

"The water smells?" He was smiling at her, obviously amused by her high jump when her cat slunk past her ankles.

"Yes. Like chlorine. Can't you still smell it in here?"

He leaned closer and drew in a slow breath, his nostrils flaring. "Nope. All I smell are flowers. Lavender, I think. Is that your shampoo?"

"It's a freesia blend, with a hint of lavender. Not shampoo. It's a body cream." For inexplicable reasons, her voice dipped embarrassingly on *cream*, and she cleared her throat.

"It's nice." He touched her skirt, so lightly she barely registered the gesture. "Flowers suit you. You're delicate."

She scoffed. "Delicate? Me? I drink Coors and watch football. I run my own business and I've even been known to dance on tables when properly motivated."

"And that means you're not delicate?"

"Delicate women need someone to take care of them." She thought of her spider episode. Sure, it would've been nice to have a guy around to get rid of the thing, but she could do it herself. Though she hadn't. Yet. "I don't."

He jutted his chin toward her sink. "So you could fix that, if you chose."

"Sure." She propped her hands on her hips as he moved slightly closer. "I can do anything I put my mind to."

"Really." More of the distance between them disappeared. Did he realize he was about to stomp on her boots? And her toes? But she had ten of them, so surely she could spare a few.

His eyes were blue, she noted a little dizzily. This close, they were the shade of the center of an anemone. The color fanned out from his pupils and got lighter at the edges, though that visual effect might've been a result of the fumes. They were probably also to blame for her sudden urge to plant her hands on his broad chest and haul him in for a kiss.

Alexa grimaced at her train of thoughts. Clearly she was now suffering from stress-based arousal transference.

A well-known sexual phenomenon, she was sure.

"I like a woman who doesn't stand around and demand

immediate service."

She didn't reply at first, because she kind of had. But this wasn't her area of expertise, and she'd had a rough day, the cherry on top of a rough year. When it came to flowers, she had it all under control. Except lately, though she had a plan to handle that.

Plans helped make negotiating life easier. Even her currently nonexistent sex life could benefit.

"There's nothing wrong with having high expectations," she said, firming her voice against its insistent wobble. That wobble hadn't been there before the last few months, and she hated it. "Just look around this place. The rates were decent and I own Divine Flowers, so I figured the building would be okay. And it's not. There are bugs in the closet and the AC's crappy and—"

He glanced past her. "I like your beaded curtain."

She frowned. "It's tacky as hell, but I didn't have anything better to hang up."

"The bed's more important than the wall hangings anyway, don't you think?"

He wasn't looking at her, just studying the apartment. As if he were considering her space and what could be done with it. "I have an air mattress," she said in a low voice, wondering if somehow he'd missed that aspect of her accommodations.

"Is it comfortable?" He rubbed the back of his neck. "Because I could probably come up with something better—"

Finally, a segue from her pity party for two into a possible sex fiesta. She wet her lips. "Are you offering me yours?"

A smile curved his insolent mouth. Clearly the question didn't shock him. Maybe strange women propositioned him daily. A man who came with such sturdy tools couldn't be that easy to find. She should know. "Would you accept if I did?"

Would she? It was one thing to consider doing something

crazy. Something else to go for it.

"The air mattress is okay," she muttered. So close and yet so far. *Wuss.* "Not that it matters. This is just temporary. Barely a pit stop."

"Oh yeah? On your way to bigger and better places?"

Though it took effort, she held his gaze as she gave him a firm nod. She'd probably just imagined that quiver in her chin. He certainly couldn't have seen it.

"You know, I think we might just get along, Alexa Conroy." She had only a moment to panic at his knowledge of her full name—first which apartment was hers, now her name, what was next?—before he flashed a dazzling grin that bumped up his looks from intriguing to *holy hell, Batman, too bad these panties aren't flame-retardant.*

When he knelt to open his toolbox, she smothered a sigh. What hands he had on him.

God, she was losing it. Now hands were turning her on. If the sex bus didn't make a stop in her valley soon, she might just lower her standards to the level of a whiskey fix. As in, she wouldn't remember the guy once the whiskey wore off. Not that she'd ever done that, but first time for everything.

As if he could hear her thoughts, his smile grew. "Now, about that leak of yours…"

$\cdots$

Unless Dillon was mistaken, the princess wanted more worked on than her pipes.

He still hadn't quite figured out why she was there. Why would someone wearing designer clothes and with a bunch of pricey furniture rent a rundown studio apartment? Apparently she planned to slum it while she drew her haughtiness around her like a cloak full of holes.

No wonder she seemed so tense.

Hell, if she was stressed now, wait until she found out the guy she'd been flirting with not only wasn't the plumber, but actually owned this building and several other income properties in downtown Haven.

More accurately, his parents owned them, but that was virtually the same thing since he and his brother, Cory, were already in the process of taking over more of their family's holdings while their parents prepared for early retirement. Those holdings included the aforementioned income properties and the chain of Value Hardware stores throughout Pennsylvania, New Jersey, and Ohio his parents had grown from two stores to ten.

Not that Dillon wanted to take over anything. Not that he held one whit of interest in being some corporate whiz kid. That was his brother's excuse for megalomania. Cory's latest project to take over the world included a lifestyle magazine that would supposedly solidify Value Hardware's position in the home beautification business. The guy probably wouldn't stop until the letters VH were embroidered on every luxe bamboo doormat across America.

He took a perverse pleasure in offering his seeming compliance with most of his older brother's plans, and then twisting them from the inside out. That included making whatever upgrades were needed to their rental properties — and not just the bare minimums either. The tenants would appreciate the new floors and improved air-conditioning, even if Cory suggested cutting corners. He had a role in the family, in the business, and he didn't shirk his duty. Or skimp on putting his wallet where his mouth was.

"Is it fixed yet?" Alexa demanded, leaning forward so that her mile-long dark hair spilled over her shoulders. She'd taken it down a little while ago, and he'd caught himself fantasizing about dragging his fingers through the tumbled brown strands more than once. Preferably while sampling her pouty raspberry lips.

"Not yet. I'll let you know."

Her indignant huff of breath made him grin. She'd asked several times already. He should find her annoying. That he didn't probably said something detrimental about his character. But along with the cute nose wrinkle she got, she had sad eyes. There was more to Alexa Conroy than what was on the surface, and already he wanted to peel back the layers.

"Are you in a hurry or something?" he asked, drawing his attention from her to the sink.

"I just don't like leaving my store in other people's care for too long."

"Because you don't trust them?"

"No, because it's my responsibility, not theirs." When he stole another glimpse of her, her expression had turned determined. She might've been willing to flirt before, but now that he hadn't managed to work miracles in minutes, she was all business.

Except for those lingering looks she occasionally coasted down his body...

Maybe that was why he was enjoying playing the part Alexa had so neatly slotted him into. Something about being in her bathroom, fixing stuff while she watched, felt right. It was also the most enjoyment he'd had in too long to remember.

Dillon James, notorious ladies' man, would have no trouble charming her into bed, and he probably wouldn't have a whole lot of remorse, either. But that wasn't who he was in Alexa's eyes. Which was exactly the problem—she didn't know the score.

He'd just fix her sink and get gone, no matter what naughty messages her now-bare, lilac-tipped toes wiggled his way as she bounced one long shapely leg over the other from her perch on the toilet. A thin chain encircled her narrow ankle, dangling charms. Purple, of course. That was her signature color. Just as that aromatic lotion she'd talked about was apparently her signature scent.

And holy shit, was it hot.

Not that it made one whit of difference. Despite her flashing blue eyes, stubborn backbone, and occasionally snide remarks, he wasn't about to blur the lines. He knew she owned the store on the first floor—and he may or may not have spent time accidentally painting windowsills in her apartment while she'd been hanging a potted arrangement from the light post in front of the building—but she had to be struggling financially if she'd moved in to the Rison.

He wasn't going to take advantage of her situation. Only a real creep would use her bad day as an opportunity to get laid.

Or a guy who hasn't had sex in months.

"Are you a licensed plumber?"

"Are you a licensed florist?" He didn't look her way, mainly because he didn't need the distraction. Or the encouragement to do really bad things he shouldn't be considering.

"Your evasiveness isn't calming my concerns."

"Neither is yours. What if I need flowers? How can I be sure you know your stuff?"

"Take a look at my shop," she snapped.

He grinned and reached for another wrench. "Take a look at my tools." When she gusted out a sigh, he relented. "Yes, I've taken classes. I have the appropriate certifications for all the work I do on this building. I also have good references."

But she wouldn't be getting them from him, unless she intended to meet his parents for reasons that extended beyond skilled plumbing work. And that wouldn't be happening.

Mercifully she stayed quiet for several minutes. When she wasn't talking, he didn't have to block out the way his mind wanted to superimpose her husky voice saying inappropriate things, preferably while they were naked. "Almost done?"

"Not yet," he said cheerfully, wiping his grimy hands on the rag he'd unearthed from his tool kit.

"Do you take this long with everything or just when you're playing with pipes?"

Oh yeah, he couldn't resist that one.

He leaned out from under the sink and cocked his head, letting his gaze roam her face as if he had all the time in the world to learn her with his eyes. "I take as much time as a project needs." He let his voice drop. "Patience pays off in ways you probably can't imagine."

As he'd hoped, her lips parted. "Sometimes fast is good enough," she said, her chest rising and falling with her breaths. Her nipples tightened, just enough to poke through her top.

Just enough to make him harder than the wrench he gripped in his fist.

"Depends what we're talking about. I like to make sure I do a thorough job." He lowered his gaze to her chest for barely an instant. "Though I can't deny some are worthy of repeats." At her hiss of breath, he flashed her a grin. "Ah well. Back to work."

"Jerk," she mumbled.

Her declaration garnered her a raised brow. "Problem?"

"No." She shook her head so vehemently his grin grew. "None at all."

Ah, he'd flustered her. Somehow he didn't think that happened often. What would she do if he amped their play up a notch? "You've given me an idea. Since you're so competent, I bet you could help me with this next part."

"Me?" She straightened and the lust drained from her

eyes. "Of course I could. What do you need?"

He pointed to the tool kit. "Grab that wrench there." When she didn't move, he smiled and pointed to the right tool. He fully expected her to roll her eyes, but she looked interested. Fascinated even.

Damn, her quick brain turned him on almost as much as her ankle bracelet. Maybe more.

"What do I do with it?"

"First I need to take off the knob on the faucet." He removed it and set it aside, then wrapped the rag around the spout. "C'mere."

She put up her hair in a quick knot, then stood next to him, her head bent, mouth pursed. "Now what?"

"We're going to remove this valve, so that I can see if the washer's in good shape."

Barely blinking, she nodded. "Okay."

"You can breathe. There are no lives at stake here, Alexa, I promise."

She jerked her chin at him. "Just do your thing, wise guy."

"Nope, you're doing it." With his free hand, he motioned to the wrench she'd picked up and grasped like a weapon. "I'm holding the spout steady, so you unscrew the washer. Okay?"

She leaned in and did as he asked, hesitantly turning it clockwise. A curl fell in her eyes and she blew it away, her focus so intent she didn't realize at first she was making the washer tighter, not looser.

He shifted behind her and placed his arm next hers to guide her hand in the opposite direction. His stomach tightened at the first contact of their skin. She smelled like summer—flowers, and sunshine, and yes, even chlorine—and he wanted to tilt his hips forward and bury his face in her hair. Not bound tightly as it was now, but loosened around her shoulders so he could use it for leverage when he—

"Oops, sorry. I was doing it wrong. Like—" She glanced over her shoulder and broke off, her question ending in a hot exhale. Her eyes narrowed as he closed his fingers over hers on the wrench. "Like this?" she asked, her voice noticeably lower. Huskier.

"Just like that. Slow and easy." He leaned in to adjust her grip and she stiffened, her curvaceous body going rigid between him and the sink.

That wasn't all that was rigid right now. Not even close.

"How long do I do this?" she asked breathlessly, arching just enough to bring her bottom hard against his erection.

He barely muffled an oath and leaned in closer, just enough that she made a noise in her throat he almost thought he'd imagined. Then she did it again. A sigh. A gasp. Some mixture of the two. He shut his eyes and gritted out, "Until I say stop."

"But I think—" She broke off and shifted restlessly against him. Bringing them flush together and wiping away the last of his good intentions.

When he flexed his hips, her hand spasmed and she whimpered as the loosened piece slipped off and fell into the bowl. He let go of the spout and stepped around her, thankfully breaking the contact of their bodies, then snatched up the part.

Damn, that had been close. Too close.

Not nearly close enough.

He moved to her side, breathing hard. Trying to remember he had ethics, somewhere down deep beneath the need churning in his gut. He cast a sideways glance at her, and they tipped toward each other like bowling pins pulled by magnets. Her lips were so close, a breath away. If he leaned in, if he just could taste her once—

At the last second, he jerked back. *Christ*. Her pupils

were dilated, her lips parted. She'd been ready for that kiss. Hell, she'd wanted it too.

In another second, he would've been in the middle of the best mistake of his life.

"Now what?" she whispered.

Dumbly, he glanced down at the part he held. What was its purpose again? Sink. Water flowing. Release.

Shit.

"Washer looks good," he said, as he rushed to put everything to rights before his shaking fingers gave him away. "Turns out I just need a part from the hardware store. Everything else is fine. I'd be happy to go get it and take care of this for you."

Operative word being "go." He'd just come *way* too close to crossing the line. As much as he wanted to taste her, he couldn't. Not until she knew he wasn't just the plumber. Not when she'd knocked him so far off his game he couldn't see straight and she didn't even know his name.

"The store?" she echoed, shutting her eyes as if she needed a moment. He understood the feeling. She took a deep breath then opened her eyes. Their sheer power nailed him square in the chest. "What store would you get the part from?"

He fought to get his brain back in gear as he rubbed his scruffy chin. "Uh, Haven's only hardware store. Val—"

She set aside the wrench and crossed her arms over her chest, a move she repeated with alarming frequency. It was probably a minor miracle she didn't have a sign across her cleavage declaring No Trespassing.

Clearly, the moment they'd shared over the sink was already ancient history.

"Don't say it." She dropped back down on the toilet, her shoulders slumping. "You are not to speak that name within these walls."

Now this was interesting. He cocked his head, waiting for her to explain herself. Had she gotten bad service at his parents' store or something? Maybe gotten a batch of bad paint? Even so, why would that make her face redden and her eyes burn? "You going to elaborate?"

"Nothing to say." Her crossed arms came up again. Naturally. "I'm just not fond of that store. At all. In fact, I think it sucks mule testicles."

He coughed and thumped his fist on his chest to get the oxygen moving again. "Haven't heard that expression before."

"It fits." She frowned and fingered the short silver chain around her neck. A long, milky stone hung from the center, drawing his gaze where it had no business going. He swiftly aimed his focus back on her face and wished he hadn't. Her direct eyes were even more dangerous than the rest of her. "I'd prefer you drive to Renault to get the part. I realize that would take longer."

Evidently his time was not her concern. Also evidently, he would not be revealing who he was anytime soon, because as soon as she realized his ties to the store that aroused so much of her ire, odd as that was, she'd likely knee him in the balls and slap him across the face. As she should. A decent, upstanding guy didn't lie to a girl just so he could kiss her brainless.

He needed to get out of her apartment before he did something he couldn't take back.

And damn sure wouldn't want to.

"By the way, you never told me your name," she said, her tone silky.

At least he could give her his name without letting the drill out of the bag. He dropped his rag into the toolbox and shut it. Then he glanced up at her sexy smile and his hand jerked on his kit. Jesus, would he ever learn not to look at what he couldn't touch? "Dillon James."

"Dillon James," she repeated, her voice a purr as she rose with the grace of a dancer. Not ballet. She wasn't that coolly antiseptic, though she tried to be. "How many tats do you have?"

"What is this, twenty questions?"

"Just curious." She indicated his upper arm. "There's one. Do you have more?"

"Yeah. A couple more. A skull, and a snake."

Interest flared across her face as she darted her gaze over his body. "Where?"

Uh-uh. *Tell* invariably led to *show*, and that wasn't happening. Even if he ached for it to. "Leave a guy some mystery, would you?"

Something dark and wicked burned in her blue eyes, riding shotgun with the pain she'd stuffed down so far she probably figured no one saw it.

He saw.

But that didn't mean he could do a damn thing about it, assuming he hadn't imagined what lurked in her expression. He had no right to ask questions that weren't the usual *getting-to-know-you* type of fare. Certainly had no cause to try to make her laugh again, just to hear that free, happy sound. To know he'd caused it, given her that moment of pleasure, egotistical bastard that he was. He cleared his throat. "I have to go." *Now*.

"You're coming back, though, right?" she asked, fingering her choker.

He hefted his toolbox. "Yeah. I'll be back." When he started to move past her, she stepped forward. His breath tripped as her hand came up to his chest. God, if she touched him right now he'd lose it.

"You forgot this." She offered him his wrench. Their gazes

collided and a slow, sly smile curved her mouth. She knew exactly what he'd been thinking. "See you later, Dillon."

"Lock up after I go," he said, then got the hell out of there.

Chapter Two

The smell of sawdust, fresh paint, and the clean and somehow aromatic scent of new plastic hit Dillon as he stepped into Value Hardware, as it always did. He could bring back that indefinable hardware store aroma in an instant, with all the happy memories of home and concerns for the future it brought.

New concerns had crowded in, and he'd come there to satisfy some of them. Where, exactly, did Alexa's hostility toward Value Hardware come from? Maybe it really was just because the two stores had some business overlap and therefore a rivalry, but he had his doubts.

When his brother was involved, anything was possible. If Alexa was feeling the squeeze from Value Hardware, Cory probably knew about it. Hell, he'd probably tightened the screws, especially considering they owned the building that housed her store. Cory wouldn't tiptoe around wanting to cut out the competition. Just not his style.

Time to find out what the deal was. Maybe in the process he'd even lose the damn erection he still hadn't been able to shake since he'd left her.

At the rate he was going, maybe he never would. He'd die hard and unfulfilled and feeling somehow cock-blocked by his shark of an older brother. Not the first time either.

He took the quickest route to his office and booted up his computer. As usual his e-mail was a hot mess, full of "urgent" things he'd already ignored for several days. They'd wait a few longer. He logged into the server and accessed his accounting program, running her name first. A genius data monkey had set up the system to cross-reference details practically down to a client's billing preference.

He grinned. Days like today he appreciated his own genius.

Too bad his grin didn't last.

She was in trouble, the kind that even a big night at the casino wouldn't touch. Notices had stacked up, their language becoming increasingly more confrontational. That they'd never crossed the line beyond what was legal was a small comfort.

Not much of one, though, when he could still smell her on his clothes. Her fragrance was a palpable thing in his office, wrapping around him until he couldn't breathe. Couldn't think.

So much for a harmless flirt-and-run. Dammit. And his day was about to get a whole lot worse, because he needed to talk to Cory.

His mistake was taking a quick loop of the store before he headed toward Cory's office. He'd needed to work off some of his frustration, and instead he got an armload of his mom.

"Sweetie!"

Dillon grinned at his mother's warm hug. "Hiya, Mom."

"You haven't lost weight, have you?" She moved back to hold him at arm's length, her blue eyes radiating worry. "You don't come over for dinner enough."

"I've been working on the apartments most nights lately. With Cory's insistence that we get them up to full occupancy, I've been scrambling to get them ready."

And apparently not succeeding, considering the sorry state of Alexa's apartment. But he'd been doing triage on the Rison's worst ones first, and hers hadn't been among them. He'd make it up to her, one way or another. If he had to slip into the place when she was at the floral shop and do the improvements piecemeal, he would.

"You could hire help. No one ever said you had to handle it all yourself. Not that you'd have any trouble, strong, strapping guy like you." She squeezed his biceps and made him laugh.

He loved hanging with her, something he hadn't been doing nearly enough of lately. He'd buried himself in fixing up their income properties and at the house he was helping to rehab for a returning veteran for more than one reason. He loved the work, true, but he was also trying to avoid—

"Such a strapping guy should have his pick of dates for the Helping Hands benefit." She tilted her head and gave him a sweet, disarming smile. Her narrowing-in-for-the-kill-you-with-kindness look. "Have you found one yet?"

That.

"Do we have to talk about this right now?" He scraped a hand over the back of his head and resisted the urge to scuff the toe of his boot along the floor. Almost thirty or not, when Corinne Santangelo gave him that look, he regressed to about fifteen in his head. Especially since he knew it was just the beginning.

"Yes, we do. It's in just a couple weeks. I know you've been tied up, sweetie, but maybe if you put half as much effort into finding a date as you did in planning the fund-raiser, you'd have a better selection of dates to pick from."

Yep, here it came. She was about to chide him about bringing what his stepfather, Raymond, called "floozies" to the event. They both claimed they just wanted him to be happy with someone who wasn't a gold digger, as the so-called floozies usually turned out to be, but he knew the company's reputation was also on the line.

As Value Hardware's primary annual fund-raising benefit, the Helping Hands charity got a lot of notice. It was Dillon's brainchild, his baby, the part of the business that made sense to him beyond the profit-and-loss statements that Cory lived and breathed. But it was also his yearly chance to remind his parents he wouldn't embrace a role in the spotlight, even if that meant hearing an earful afterward about whom he selected to accompany him.

Plus, he'd discovered one indisputable fact—"bad" girls were better in bed. So shoot him.

"I'm sure I'll be able to find someone." He smothered a grin. Whether she approved of his choice, however…

His parents were picky. If he didn't bring just the right kind of woman to the event to get his folks off his back, pretty soon they'd start setting him up on blind dates with "suitable" women he didn't even want to share a meal with, never mind seriously date.

He'd gone out with those women before. Ones who pretended to really enjoy watching the sun set on a rickety old fishing boat, at least until they thought they had him snagged. *He* was the prime catch, not the fish.

"Uh-huh." She waved at a passing customer and chitchatted for a moment about an arthritic poodle, then returned her attention to Dillon. "I'm onto you, kid."

"Oh really?"

"Come back to my office."

Uh-oh. Not good. Office talks were only one step better

than when she called him by his full name. "I have this part I need to get—" *And some questions I need to ask your* other *son.*

"It'll keep for a few minutes."

Smiling at more customers, she led the way down the power tools aisle. She inspired waves of greeting in almost everyone she passed. Such was her magic. Just because he didn't think he was cut out for the corporate blueprint didn't mean he couldn't appreciate all the hard work his mom and stepfather had put into making the company a success.

People stopped him as well, and he couldn't say he minded talking tools. Haven was a small, close-knit town, and he'd known many of these people since he'd been in diapers. The three years he'd spent living in New Jersey had been a welcome getaway, but he'd always known he'd come back. This was his legacy.

Once they reached the back of the store, they bypassed Dillon's own closet-sized office and continued on to her larger one. At the end of the hall were his stepfather's office and Cory's lair. It was easy to differentiate the two. From Raymond's open door came the low tones of the Beatles' *White Album,* whereas Cory never played music. He also never opened his door.

His mom led him inside her office, then circled her wide carved rosewood desk to take a seat behind it. The room held all the touches of home—framed pictures, a soft, knitted blanket over the back of her chair for when the AC made it too cold, a few thriving plants. Even the sea-green walls made the space seem soothing rather than like an office.

But Dillon still knew what it was. And every time he locked himself inside one of these enlarged coffins, he couldn't stop thinking about everything he was missing. Sunshine. Fresh air. The burn of his muscles as the hours passed in a blur of exertion.

She leaned forward, her auburn bob swinging against her jaw. Though she and her husband were near retirement, something they told everyone who would listen, she fought the battle against gray hair and wrinkles with steely determination. "Dad and I want to sit down with you and your brother sometime in the next few weeks."

Though outwardly he gave her a calm nod, inwardly his stomach clenched. It was too soon. They'd made him think there was time before he'd have to assume the reins along with Cory, and from her expression, there clearly wasn't.

If their retirement was progressing faster than Dillon had assumed while he'd been up to his elbows in copper pipes and linoleum, that meant Cory had to be drowning in paperwork. Not that he'd complain or ask for help. He'd seethe. His older brother was an expert at that.

When she gripped her hands together, his petty concerns fell away. "Is everything okay?"

"Yes. Yes," she repeated as he edged forward on his seat. "Everything's fine. Dad's asthma is a bit worse than it was."

"Is he all right? He never said anything—"

"He's fine," she soothed, giving him a reassuring smile. "But since we're looking at retirement anyway, his doctor recommended we try a different climate. Dry air would help his condition, we're told, so we're considering a move."

"To where?"

"A few places are on the list. Scottsdale's leading it."

"Scottsdale, Arizona?" Across the country? "What about the house?" And his mom's horse, and the acreage, and… Christ, a clusterfuck of a headache was about to pound through his left eye.

"Yes, Arizona. If we decide to move, we'll be putting the house up for sale, unless one of you boys wants it."

Dillon snorted. "Cory lives in the biggest penthouse in Haven. You honestly think he'd give a rat's ass about tending some chickens and a horse? He'll sell Misty before you're on the plane." The sadness he glimpsed in her eyes shut him up, and fast.

"Cory knows his duty," she said quietly.

Alexa flashed into his mind. Her smile. Her brief laugh. Especially her weary blue eyes. Did Cory's duty include antagonizing dedicated small-business owners struggling to stay afloat?

And if so, he'd be shouldering that duty alone, because Dillon would have no part.

"Yeah, and I don't." He worked his jaw as he stared out the window beside her desk, noting the mocking cluster of smiley-face balloons by the welcome sign out front. Everyone was welcome at Value Hardware. His family had embraced the community, and in turn the community had embraced them.

"You're not like your brother, and your dad and I understand that. You've always wanted to do your own thing. That's why you kept Tommy's name when your brother took Raymond's. You never—"

"That's not why."

"No?" She appeared genuinely curious.

"No. I didn't want Tommy to think we were both abandoning him." Saying it aloud, knowing it was sterling truth, made him grind his teeth.

It figured he'd effectively excluded himself from his family to try to show solidarity with a man who thought being a dad meant visiting once a year on birthdays and giving his boys magazine subscriptions for Christmas—Cory got *Sports Illustrated*; Dillon got *Popular Mechanics*.

His mother sighed and rubbed her temple. Maybe he'd

somehow telepathically shared his headache. "You're a good boy, Dill. You always have been. You've also always been incredibly stubborn."

"Me?"

"Yes, you." With her smile, the thread of tension in the room eased. "You're a rebel, baby, with the motorcycle to prove it. And the tattoos. Don't you remember when you came home with that tribal thing on your arm and tried to convince me it was the greatest thing ever?" She shook her head, still smiling fondly. "Wings so you'd never be stuck in any one place."

"I remember." As a teenager, he'd chosen tattoos he probably wouldn't now. But those markers on his body were permanent reminders of who he'd been—and who he wanted to be.

She reached out to straighten one of the family photos scattered across her desk. The one she touched was of Dillon and Cory as kids, standing in front of the paddock behind their family house. Arms around each other's shoulders, grins as wide as the sky.

It had been years since they'd been that close. There had been a time in high school when they'd even talked about going to the same college, but that had disappeared after the differences growing roots between them had choked most of the friendship out of their relationship. Eventually Dillon had headed to NYU to study business with a focus on corporate social responsibility, and Cory had gotten an MBA from Wharton.

His idea of heaven was several hours on his bike, winding through the Pennsylvania mountainside with no agenda. Or venturing to the roof of the Rison to look out over the city and think. Not making plans to take over the world and glad-handing like Cory. Not sitting down for cozy fireside chats like his parents. Helping others—through his charity work, or hell, even when he assisted a customer at the store—made him happy, but when the world got to be too much, he escaped with his fishing pole to the lake. He wasn't lonely, most of the time. The absence of people meant no expectations. And no chance of not meeting them.

When the silence stretched, she sighed. "Sweetie, Cory's Cory and you're you. Your dad and I love you, just the way you are." She rose and came around the desk, then cupped his cheek in her hand. "Fighting to show everyone what you're not isn't going to prove your worth. Only you can do that." Her smile was indulgent. "Someday you'll realize."

When he rose, she enfolded him in a healing hug, saturating him in her comforting rosewater and vanilla scent.

"Let me know when you want me at the house." He nearly groaned at the sound of the door across the hall opening and shutting with a slam. Cory on his way out, no doubt, which meant there'd be no cornering him about Alexa today. "I'll be there."

"I will, just as soon as we wrangle up that workaholic brother of yours." She stepped back and patted his cheek. "I love you, Dill. You'll always be my baby boy."

Though the back of his neck prickled uncomfortably with embarrassment, her words settled in his chest. There it was, the acceptance he'd always sought. All he had to do was figure out how to take it.

"Love you, too." He kissed her cheek and headed for the door. "I'll see you soon."

"Don't forget your part," she called.

His mind shot back to Alexa. She and her business were in serious trouble, and he wanted to help her. Hell, he wanted *her*, period, more than he'd counted on when she'd knocked on the door of the Kelly apartment. Much more than he had any woman in too long to remember.

Change was coming. Time to seize the day, and everything that came with it.

"Think I may have to head out to Renault for it, actually." He smiled and shut the door behind him.

. . .

"Are you going to stop stabbing that steak and actually eat some of it?"

Alexa glanced up at her best friend Nellie's question. "I'm tenderizing it," she said, setting down her fork to reach for her iced tea.

Considering Nellie had said dinner was her treat, she didn't want to seem ungrateful. She also hadn't had steak in months and probably wouldn't again for just as long. Too bad her appetite waxed and waned like the phases of the moon these days.

"You're bummed about selling the house, huh?"

"No." Alexa went back to her steak, being careful to cut the meat into small slices. She'd underestimated how much nervous energy she had to burn tonight. A lot of that had to do with her studly plumber and her near miss with his delectable lips. Dillon must be one of those moral *can't kiss during the first home improvement project* types. "My decision to sell was the right one. I know my new place will be awesome after I do some decorating."

Once the imminent flood threat is gone…

Nellie frowned and leaned forward, stopping short when her oversized belly bumped the edge of the table. "Still not used to this," she muttered, rubbing her stomach.

Alexa laughed. "You've only been pregnant for five months now. Why would you be used to it yet?"

"Funny. It changes your center of balance or something. I keep thinking I'm smaller than I am." She shrugged, but it didn't diminish her beaming smile.

Everyone in the world, it seemed, was happy. Alexa's older brother, Jake, certainly was, with his and Nellie's little girl on the way. They'd settled into domestic bliss with a suddenness Alexa still wasn't sure she'd caught up to. She was thrilled for them, of course, but she couldn't help looking around her world sometimes and wondering when it had tilted off its axis.

Less than two years ago she and Nellie had been single, freewheeling women, only planning as far as the next Friday night. Then Nellie and Jake had gotten married. Shortly thereafter, Roz Keller, Alexa's boss, mentor, and the woman who'd owned Divine for twenty years, died. And she'd left the shop—and all its overdue bills—to Alexa.

Overnight, she'd gone from a flower designer to a business owner. That it had happened at the height of the recession hadn't helped. While her brother and Nellie were building their love nest outside of town, she'd been delving into the books and discovering exactly how much Roz had hidden behind comforting pats on the back when Alexa voiced concerns about the drop-off in customers.

As fast she could say *financial ruin*, Alexa's former champagne taste had morphed into a miserly dedication to pinching pennies. Now she funneled all her extra money into the shop. Luckily she already had a great wardrobe. Outwardly she still looked every bit the confident, successful young businesswoman.

Inside, however, she was shaking in her fancy lingerie.

"Lex?" Nellie reached out to grip Alexa's wrist. "Honey, are you all right?"

"I'm fine." She would be. The first step in achieving that would be to get her mind off her problems, especially the ones she'd already made a plan to fix.

"Are you sure? If you want to talk, I'm happy to listen. I won't even interrupt." The corner of Nellie's mouth lifted. "Much."

"I'm good, thanks." Okay, not really. But at least there had been one notable bright spot to her day, and he was over six feet tall and boasted enough muscles to feed her most lurid fantasies for months.

"Okay, fine." Nellie let out an exaggerated sigh. "Then tell me what's new with you."

Alexa swallowed a bite of fluffy mashed potatoes and decided she might as well get some entertainment out of the day's events. "I almost kissed my plumber. Or he almost kissed me. Not really sure."

Nellie coughed and set down her heaping forkful of macaroni and cheese. "Excuse me?"

"He's a plumber in my new building." Alexa dragged a sliver of meat through steak sauce. These days she was full before she made it halfway through a meal. Damn stress. "He didn't get riled at me, though I was a little keyed up."

"You? Keyed up? Impossible. So, uh, why would you almost kiss a strange man?"

Why indeed. The intensely hot moments she'd spent with Dillon in her bathroom might as well have shone a spotlight on her sexual drought. From where she was sitting, rushing headlong into an impetuous blink-and-its-over fling with a man who was likely all wrong for her was made of win. Assuming she could get Dillon on board, which might require some finesse considering his disappearing act.

She'd just have to convince him. Through tactical—and explicit—means.

"Do you remember the old Alexa?" she asked, meeting Nellie's concerned hazel gaze. "The one who grabbed hold of the Tilt-A-Whirl of life and held on with both hands?"

"The one who had a love life I was always jealous of? Yeah, I remember her. But you've grown up now."

"So if you grow up, you can't enjoy yourself anymore? You can't snatch a few hours from real life and go do something wild and crazy, just so you don't forget you still can?" The memory of Dillon pressed so tight against her back, hard and hot, drew forth a shiver she couldn't suppress. Why the hell hadn't she hadn't taken her own advice?

"Life's about more than staying up at night crunching numbers you can't make balance, no matter what you do," she continued, softer now, as she shifted her gaze to the twisted stems of the yellow and peach carnations in the table vase. So pretty and simple. But right now, carnations represented everything she hadn't yet made work. "Or it should be."

"I know you've had a rough time lately. You don't have to stay up alone. Ever. Besides, I can't sleep much now that munchkin likes to pretend she's rolling down the Falls in a barrel." Nellie gave her a beseeching look that any man, woman, or child would have trouble saying no to. "Call me and we'll watch reality TV together. Or trash-talk men. I'm always up for that."

Alexa rolled her eyes. "You're completely, disgustingly, in love with my brother. You haven't trashed him once, ever. Not to mention the last three times I've been over you were lights out, blankie up to the neck, by nine o'clock."

"Hey, I'm trying to help. I know I can't necessarily relate to everything you're going through right now, but true friends stick by you and try to offer moral support."

Alexa sighed at Nellie's hurt tone. Great. Any time now she'd make the pregnant lady cry and her saintly brother Jake would swoop in and tell her off. As he probably should.

Surely she needed *someone* to tell her off. She'd been

snippy and tense with everyone lately. "I'm sorry, Nellie-cakes. I had no reason to snap at you," she said, reaching out to clasp Nellie's hand.

"No. You didn't. But I accept the apology." Nellie smiled and reached behind her to grab her jacket off the back of her chair. "Sheesh, the AC in here is crazy. I'm freezing!"

"Aww, don't cover up the fuzzy gray kitten," Alexa protested, laughing at the narrow-eyed look she got in return.

Nellie—Noelle to those who hadn't been her best friend since they were in kindergarten—had a tendency to wear shirts adorned with sheep and bunnies under the best of circumstances, but pregnancy had given her the chance to go all out. Designers of maternity clothes evidently loved the animal theme. Today's shirt featured an adorable tabby cat holding up a daisy.

Another flower. God, no wonder she couldn't escape her thoughts. Divine's eviction bill would probably arrive with a tulip stamp on the envelope.

"Not all of us are meant to wear designer clothes," Nellie said with a sniff as she bundled her jacket around herself. But the teasing light was back in her eyes, letting Alexa know the crisis had passed.

If luck held, there would be no crying fits at their dinner table, either hormonally or situationally based. All things considered, that meant they were doing okay.

She was doing okay.

"So tell me more about your plumber," Nellie said, returning to her dinner. She ate with a gusto that Alexa couldn't help but envy. Truthfully, there were a lot of things about Nellie's life she envied, when she dared admit it to herself.

Which wouldn't be tonight. Settling down was all well and good for some people, but not her. Who wanted to stare at the same guy's mug day in and day out? Who wanted the tiny noose of a gold band around their finger? Not her. She wanted sex. Dirty, potentially regrettable sex. With Dillon.

"He's not my plumber." Giving up on her half-eaten meal, Alexa reached for the dessert menu. She was in a chocolate sort of mood. "He could've been, for an hour or so. Maybe two, depending on the size of his wrench."

"Lex!"

Alexa giggled and peered at her best friend over the top of her menu. "Split some chocolate lava cake with me?"

"As if you had to ask. So what's his name?"

"Dillon James." Alexa went back to looking at the menu. She could always drown her sorrows in apple brown betty. With extra whipped cream, nutmeg, and a sprinkling of walnuts. "Or would you rather—"

"Dillon? Is he new in town?"

Alexa was tempted to respond with *how should I know* but decided that might make her look sort of indiscriminate. Nellie had never even kissed a guy she didn't have a full dossier on, so it wouldn't take much to squick her out. "I have no idea."

"Hmm." Nellie shoveled in more mac and cheese, then rested her chin on her palm. "Dillon's a yummy name. Is he yummy?"

"He's attractive."

"Attractive tells me nothing. Less than nothing." Nellie did her typical pouty mouth thing that turned Jake into a salivating mess. Luckily Alexa wasn't similarly afflicted. "You won't give up the goods to the fat, married, pregnant lady?"

"Who you calling fat?" Grinning, Jake came up behind Nellie and bent to kiss her forehead. "Not my gorgeous wife, I hope."

Nellie laughed and thrust herself at Jake with enough

force to bowl him over had his feet not been securely planted. "You must've gotten my message."

"I did, and I rushed home from my business trip just to eat dinner with my two favorite people." He came around the table to Alexa and gave her a teasing smile. "No hug for your big brother?"

"It's only been a week since I've seen you." But Alexa grinned just the same as she half-stood to give him a quick squeeze.

"A very long week," Nellie added, her face softening as it always did around Jake. "And it's your three favorite people. Not two."

Though it shamed her to snort, Alexa couldn't help it. She adored them, but lately even finding a decent guy to have a very indecent night with felt like climbing Mount Everest in spike heels. At this rate, she had no hope of finding what those two had.

Or even a reasonable facsimile.

"Very true." Jake smiled and thanked the waitress who bustled over to add another chair to their table. He took a seat and grabbed the menu she offered, his attention clearly on his stomach as usual. "So what're we talking about?"

"Your sister wanting to lip-lock her new plumber."

"Seriously, Nellie, if you weren't pregnant I'd—"

"Do go on," Jake said smoothly, cocking a brow. "I'm curious. Also curious about this plumber. Who is he? Do I know him?"

"*She* doesn't even know him." Nellie twirled her hair then let out a long sigh at Alexa's sharp glance. "Look, it's not that exciting in my corner of the world. I take my thrills where I can get them. Your love life thrills me."

"What love life? It's been positively stagnant lately."

"Good," Jake put in, his brows knitted. "The last thing I

want is to get another call at 2:00 a.m. because your car died at some guy's house that you barely know."

"That was in college," Alexa said under her breath, her face going hot. "And I did so know him. He was my chemistry partner."

"And he just *loved* to study after hours," Nellie teased. "Didn't you ace that course?"

"Doing extra credit always helps," Jake added with a grin.

Shaking her head, Alexa motioned for the waitress. Dessert time. Maybe bourbon time too. "God, you're so… *married*."

They both laughed, and luckily soon forgot all about her nonexistent love life in the stream of baby chatter and gossip. But Alexa's sour mood remained.

Two hours later, she let herself into her stuffy apartment. Nellie and Jake had gone back to their place to likely engage in some conjugal married bliss—*ick*—and now the night stretched in front of her, full of possibilities.

Full of nothing. As blah as her new home.

With a sigh, she tested the bathroom sink and nothing untoward happened. Had her mysterious plumber snuck in here and fixed it for real when she'd been out? Picked the lock maybe? Shimmied in through the window from the fire escape?

She looked down to see Trixie staring at her, wild-eyed. Either she was on the verge of a kitty meltdown or she was hungry, which made more sense since Alexa had yet to set out bowls of dry food and water.

After handling that, she grabbed the lone item in her refrigerator—an unopened bottle of Moscato. Snagging a paper cup, she poured herself some wine. Maybe she'd do some reading on her phone before going to sleep. Assuming she could.

At least she'd put on the sheets earlier, so all she had to do was turn out the lights and crawl under her favorite soft throw. She'd go shopping for a daybed soon enough, but until then, her air mattress would do just fine.

She was *not* a princess. She was a survivor, and she—*and* Divine—would make it.

Smiling at her new sense of resolve, she turned on her phone and saw she had two new voice mails. Great. Probably her mom with a fresh guilt trip. She'd been bugging Alexa to go shopping with her, and Alexa knew she'd only be able to put her off for so long. As if she had spare money to shop. But she could make the time and she would.

"Hi, Alexa, this is Patty. I hoped you'd be available so I didn't have to leave a message, but I'll just say it straight out. I got the mail today and there was an overdue rent notice."

Fabulous. Having her new designer see yet another overdue notice was *not* good. God, she'd thought she'd paid enough last month to make a dent in the amount she was behind. And she'd pay more just as soon as the money from the sale of her house arrived.

"I like you a lot and I enjoy my job, but I was offered a position at Value Hardware and I took it. I hope you understand. I wish you all the best—"

Alexa clicked off. After checking the other message and determining that it was her father who'd called with the guilt trip this time rather than her mother—he'd fretted ever since she'd announced she was moving into the "rat trap" above Divine—she tossed her phone aside.

Her dad could worry about the nonexistent rats and Patty could show up or not in the morning. It didn't really matter.

She was fucked.

She'd believed, wrongly it seemed, that her house closing would be the lowlight of her month. Maybe even year. Then she'd experienced some sparks with a guy who hadn't been able to get out of her place fast enough. He probably thought she was just one shade above destitute and therefore too much trouble.

Not that Dillon's opinion mattered. They didn't know each other. It wasn't as if she was looking for a boyfriend, just a lover. Someone to hold her for a little while, to remind her she was a woman.

Now this.

Clearly the universe intended to make sure she got its message. And that message was: *you suck.*

Swallowing hard, she reached for her wine and downed the cup in a few sips. She looked around her apartment, still in a state of disarray, boxes and suitcases everywhere, and jumped to her feet. Uh-uh. She couldn't stay locked up in here tonight, staring at the silver streaks of rain just beginning to slip down the windows. If she didn't get some air and some perspective, she'd lose what was left of her mind.

She went into the bathroom and freshened her makeup, though she had no idea where she was going to go. Hitting a bar sounded about as appealing as staying home. Nellie and Jake were probably halfway through a welcome home celebration. Double ick.

Occasionally on nice nights after work, she'd escape upstairs to the roof, just to check out the sunset. It was so quiet up there, and the expansive view somehow helped put her chaotic mind at ease. But she hadn't been up there in months—no sunset could soothe what ailed her now—and it was raining. Still, even sitting out in a nice, warm rain was better than sweating to death in her stiflingly hot apartment. Anything was.

She glanced down at her simple black sleeveless sheath dress. Yeah, that wouldn't work. Good thing she'd bought a pair of shorts for moving. Since she'd moved into Dante's Inferno, she had a feeling she'd be buying more.

Five minutes later, after changing into her cutoff shorts and a tight tank top she usually wore to bed, she retied her braid and grabbed her purse. The sound of the rain was now a steady patter, much heavier than it had been even a few minutes ago.

Maybe this wasn't such a good idea. Then again, did she have any better ones?

She followed the bend in the hallway to the roof access point she'd discovered about a year earlier when she'd first explored the building. Her insatiable curiosity had led her to the partially open door, held open with a doorstop to provide additional airflow to the top floor on a sweltering summer day. Unsurprisingly the door was cracked again, held open with that same heavy doorstop. Rain spattered through the opening.

Nerves crawled up her spine. Was someone up there? She glanced down at her unrestrained chest. Should she have worn a bra?

Screw it. This was a safe building. She'd worked in it for years with no problems. Despite her father's concerns about rats, there was nothing to fear, animal or human.

Right.

She toed aside the doorstop and stepped onto the narrow staircase. Her gaze swung to the top of the stairs as someone stepped into the space, blocking the remaining light.

The door behind her swung shut.

Chapter Three

"Who's up there?"

From the top of the stairs, Dillon didn't speak. He'd seen Alexa's face in the flash of light from the hallway, but up on the roof it was pretty damn dark, hence her confusion.

He didn't have any, though. She'd been on his mind all frigging day, and seeing her again when he'd finally started to focus on work —all right, not really—really pissed him off.

Other, less discriminating parts of him weren't quite so irritated.

What was she doing up here? And why hadn't he noticed her car pull up? He'd passed her in the parking lot when he'd come back with her part, and he'd decided to wait around for a couple hours to see if she returned rather than letting himself in her place to fix it. It wasn't as if he didn't have plenty of work to take care of in the building.

But after almost two hours laying flooring, he'd been desperate for some fresh air. Plus the heat meant the potted trees would need some water, so he'd filled his watering can and come upstairs. About five minutes before it started to rain.

He took a deep breath to give himself another moment, and her scent shot right past his brain to his already waking cock.

Fuck.

"It's me." *Duh. She only met you once.* He cleared his throat. "Dillon."

"Dillon?" As if she didn't believe him, she charged up the steps and stopped two below the top, wincing as rain sprayed into her face. "What're you doing up here?"

"Maintenance stuff," he said shortly, turning sideways to make room for her to shimmy past him onto the roof. The space was pretty big and surrounded by a concrete wall made even higher by the growth of shrubbery along the top. He'd been working up there for months, trying out some of the green ideas he'd been learning about online. It wasn't much to look at yet, but eventually the vegetation on the roof would help with heating and cooling the building, along with being ecologically friendly.

No one knew what he was doing up there. Not his parents, not Cory. His brother would've laughed his ass off, especially if he'd learned the amount of time Dillon had spent investigating the options. Then there was building the rooftop garden itself, which took its share of time as well. Selecting the right plants, learning about drainage systems, making it look more like an organized plan rather than a hodgepodge of shrubs and trees.

Shrubs and trees she was now staring at. Silently. Any time now she'd roll her eyes and his annoyance would skyrocket into the red zone.

"Uh, it's raining," he said, opening the door wider. "We should get downstairs."

She turned back to him, the tilt of her stance stealing his weather preparedness speech from his data banks. Right then he could be split open and seared like a filet mignon and he'd probably die thinking about the deep vee of Alexa's skinny tank top.

Damn, she had a smokin' figure. Gorgeous breasts outlined in tight purple cotton and a pert little ass in even tighter denim. He'd been up against that ass, and he wanted those breasts in his hands. In his mouth.

"You did this?" she asked.

He frowned at the way she waved her hand at his half-finished garden. "So what if I did?" He swiped the hem of his damp T-shirt over his equally damp face. All he could think about was slipping those skimpy straps off her shoulders and feasting on her skin, and she wanted to talk trees?

Florist or not, he was willing to bet she hadn't done the research he had about how bamboo and green plants were—

She moved whip-fast, slamming her hands on his chest and him against the door before his brain caught up. The watering can clattered onto the ground. She spared it a brief, puzzled glance, then fisted her hands in his T-shirt and arched up, her mouth coming closer—

Fuck it.

He fused his mouth to hers, and dammit, it was even better than he'd expected. She didn't yield to him but struggled a bit, as if she was shocked he'd taken over. That made it even hotter. He slanted his lips over hers when her startled squeak granted him access to the warm sweetness inside. *Perfect.* He took full advantage of her surprise to explore her with long, slow licks of his tongue.

Maybe his head couldn't compute what was happening, but his body sure could. He cupped her ass and rocked his hips against hers, all too aware of his violent reaction to her nearness. His dick still hadn't recovered from their bump-and-grind in her bathroom and apparently had no trouble asserting its readiness to play. Recovered now, she didn't shy away, and instead rubbed against him, her curves sliding against him in a way that had him groaning and pulling back so hard he thunked his head on the closed door.

He couldn't do this. Oh, God, he had to. She was going wild against him, and he didn't have any defenses against his hunger for her. Not when he wanted nothing more than this. Just this.

"What are we doing?" he managed as she dragged her lips down his Adam's apple. Stars danced in his vision and hell if he knew if they were from the head jolt or from their kiss.

She didn't answer him, just skated her hands down his torso and under his shirt. And what hands they were. She seemed to be touching him *everywhere*. He clung to her ass as if she was his only port in the storm, and sure enough, a bolt of lightning sizzled overhead followed by a crack of thunder. But Alexa never paused. He'd become her canvas and her fingers were her paintbrush. She sketched every ridge of muscle, every line of bone. And then the column of his cock, wedged tight into his jeans. She touched him with confidence and skill, the kind that would soon have him driving his hands into her hair and pushing her to her knees if she didn't stop.

But a woman like her wasn't meant for a quick fuck against a door, even if that was what she acted like she wanted. Even if he longed for her so much that he didn't care about anything but stealing this moment and making it theirs. He must be misreading her signals, though he was pretty adept at picking up sexual cues. Or else he'd sent some crazy ones of his own.

"Alexa." Though it took all his faculties just to get out that one word, she ignored him. Completely.

She cupped him and nipped his jaw, her teeth offering a sharp counterpoint to her palm's soft touch. His shaft lurched in her hold and she let out a delighted purr.

"Lex," he tried again, her name ending in a moan. "You don't know who I am."

He expected her to stiffen, to look up at him with those huge bluebell eyes he'd gone a little nuts for the first time he'd looked at her. She didn't.

"Alexa, listen to me." He wrapped her braid around his hand and tugged up her head, something sharp dislodging inside him the instant their gazes clashed. In the waning light, he could just make out the lust on her finely boned face. It transformed her somehow, changed her from someone he should protect—from him—into a woman he needed at all costs. "You don't understand."

She didn't. Hell, at the moment, he didn't either. Because he didn't feel like he was lying or hiding anything. He wanted to strip away the barriers between them, and this was the best way he knew how. Words were unnecessary, the language of miscommunication. Kisses and long looks and sultry touches—that was the truth, and she was the only one he could share it with.

Right now who he really was didn't matter. She knew the important stuff. He was a guy. She was a woman. Certain areas were meant to fit together. Who even cared who his family was? Maybe she really didn't even hate the hardware store. Maybe she had a secret girl-crush on it and went in there every day to fondle all the trusty hammers and saws…

Yep, he needed help. The kind he'd find alone by himself, far, far from distractions with anklets and eyes as big as moons.

"*You* don't understand," she whispered, gripping the back of his neck. She was tall for a woman, and even in flats she could reach all the important parts with only a modicum of stretching. "I don't want to know who you are. I don't care. All I want is for you to make me come."

Okay, yeah, that sent his brain on hiatus. His conscience packed its bags too. *Forget it, buddy. You're on your own now.*

"Don't say I didn't try to warn you," he said against her temple.

"I won't say anything about tonight again. Just fuck me and we'll move on. It'll be like it never happened." Out here, her eyes were darker and more luminous. They were filled with desire, definitely, but they were tinged with sadness too. And desperation. They pulled him in so deep there was only one answer he could give.

Except his cock ached so much he couldn't say anything at all. So he showed her.

He pulled on her braid and jerked her against him, absorbing her gasp with his mouth. His tongue swept between her parted lips and claimed hers, drawing her into an urgent thrust-and-retreat. All the while he sculpted her ass in his hands, massaging gently. First through her shorts, then beneath once he'd undone the zipper and slipped inside.

He hissed upon meeting the thin strip of fabric between her cheeks, somehow not surprised she'd gone the thong route. Her flesh burned his palms, hotter than even the rain that now pelted them with the force of countless tiny nails. But she was all he could feel, all he could taste as they consumed each other with ravenous kisses. She'd had wine and only now did it register in his brain, the crisp, fruity notes of it. And more, something chocolaty and rich. Or maybe that was just her, sweet and luscious all the way to the center. A deception for the senses, so that by the time he realized he was caught, it was too late. She had him.

And, oh shit, did she have him. Lock, stock, and fully loaded barrel, ready to blow.

Her hands were on his cock, working it in rough pulls through his jeans. He yanked down the shoulder of her tank top and feasted on the swell of flesh that plumped over the top, using his tongue to trace her damp nipple. Slick with rain, fragrant with her summery floral scent. Sunshine in the middle of the storm.

She made a choked sound as she latched onto his scalp with her nails, her other hand still busy between them. Impatient, he pulled the fabric down so that her breast popped over the top and into his waiting mouth.

A scrape of teeth, a hard suck, and she was writhing against him, the jerks of her hips against his already-straining shaft adding an unintended friction that made him pant.

When he couldn't take it anymore, when even the ozone-stung air burned his raw throat, he seized hold of her hips and turned her to face the door, caging her between him and the wood with his arms and his body. He scissored his teeth over the soft flesh of her neck while he spanned his hands across her waist. She felt so good in his arms, a live wire quivering with energy. "Still want this?" he whispered, his tongue zeroing in on the hollow behind her earlobe.

"God, yes. More than ever." She reached back to grab his ass, hauling him so close that they slammed together against the door. "Put your hands on me. All over me."

He stretched his fingers, teasing her with their nearness to the open zipper of her shorts. "I'm already touching you." He wanted his mouth on her, everywhere. Wanted to hear her scream.

"Not enough." She grabbed his hand and dragged him down where she wanted him, holding him between her thighs so that he could feel the heat throbbing through the denim. "Dammit."

The hissed curse instead of a plea made him grin and relent. He dove inside and drew a finger through the moisture that awaited him, flicking the edge of his fingertip over her swollen flesh. She was soaked inside and out, her own inferno as relentless as the storm that bore down on them.

"Beautiful." He pulled her earlobe between his teeth, her stud earring clinking against his teeth. Bit down when she moaned. "Make those noises for me."

She complied eagerly, and her uninhibited sounds drove him insane. He nipped her lobe again, eliciting more of her whimpers, and finally gave her a taste of what she begged for.

With a circle of his finger she stilled in his arms. With another she came back to life, clutching him deeper. Tempting him with small rocks of her pelvis. Drawing him to claim her there, first with his fingers, then his cock. That last joining would be both the beginning and their end.

Don't go there. Not now.

He stroked her sex as slowly as the raging need inside him would allow, letting his want flow out through his touch and into her willing body. If he made this good for her, if she got the orgasm she'd sought, he'd be able to sleep tonight. Giving her the release—and the escape—she craved would feed his own urges. And hopefully, vanquish them entirely in her direction.

This was his turf, both literally and metaphorically, and she couldn't knock him off his stride here. He wouldn't let her.

He pumped two fingers into her and sucked on the side of her neck, dimly realizing he would mark her skin. Some petty, elemental part of him *wanted* to brand her. For this fleeting moment, he could call her his. And could make sure she saw him on her when she looked in the mirror tomorrow, no matter what she told herself about what they'd been to each other.

Her pleasure seeped into his skin, torturing him more than the divots of driving rain he shielded her from. The hard nub beneath his thumb pulsed with her growing excitement, but it was her moans that led him on, taking him to the edge with her breathy, dirty demands.

"Get me off. I'm so close. Can you feel it?" He just barely heard her over the rush of the wind, but the words lanced into his gut and twisted coils of desire around his balls.

"I feel everything." Too much, all rushing at him with the speed of an avalanche. If he didn't jump out of the way, he'd get buried. It was an odds game, calculating how much she could take. How much he could stand.

Dillon squeezed his eyes shut and dragged her back against him, grinding his painfully stiff cock into the crease of her ass. Desperate for something to give him some relief. To build the pressure more, until one of them broke.

She squeezed him, her inner walls starting to spasm. "God, I'm gonna—"

"No." His gruff denial cut her off. He wouldn't go easy on her. Maybe other men leaped to do her bidding—he totally didn't blame them—but he'd be damned if he helped her forget him. "Not yet."

She whimpered when he drew his thumb away from her clit, his fingers never letting up inside. "Yes yet. Now," she breathed at his sharp tug on her braid.

"No," he repeated. He nuzzled her shoulder while he lowered his hand to her breast, still distended over her shirt. The beaded nipple pressed into his palm and he plucked at it, hard; gauging from the noises she made she wanted rough more than soft. Appearances could be deceiving, and this woman who made her living with flowers seemed to crave the dark and lewd with the same ferociousness he did. As she proved when he flicked her clit and she nearly went off, her body lunging forward until she banged her forehead against the door.

"You want it?" he grated against her cheek.

He wanted her to beg, to say it in no uncertain terms. She didn't give in. But her drenched, throbbing flesh told him, especially when he released her breast to fumble in his back pocket for his wallet. She grew wetter, more pliant. More ready for him to take what she so eagerly gave.

She snatched his wallet and searched through it in silence, her heavy breaths the only sign she ached as much as he did. His fingers picked up their pace inside her as she ripped the foil packet between her teeth, then passed it back with an accompanying proprietary stroke. His neglected cock jumped and she let out a throaty laugh, the sound of a woman who knew she had him under her spell. "Guess *you* want it?"

"You know I do." He couldn't help his growl, any more than he could stop himself from yanking down his jeans and boxers so he could torture her with a little skin-on-skin contact before he suited up. She slicked her hand up and down, coasting on the trickle of arousal that slipped free. Under her touch it multiplied, until he had to drop his head back and stare up at the seething gray sky.

If he'd had the energy to look around, he would've seen the world stretched out around them. Twinkling lights. Shadowy trees and hills. Buildings rising up out of the ground. As close as they seemed from up here, they might as well have been a million miles away from the web they'd spun around themselves, binding them together in the dark.

He twisted his fingers free of her snug heat and used the wet to outline her lips. She didn't balk, and instead darted out her tongue to sample what he'd left behind.

"Goddamn, woman."

She taunted him with a wiggle of her ass. "Fuck me already."

With one pull, he had her shorts and panties down, baring her pale cheeks to his hungry gaze. He wanted to see more of her. Everything. Right now he'd have to settle for feeling her, inch by inch.

He jerked on the condom with shaking fingers and stilled her sensuous movements with a shallow thrust before he pulled out and left her wanting. Then again and again, going slightly deeper, just enough to earn her ragged breaths and the pinch of her nails into his ass.

God, what he wouldn't give to feel that bite of pain down his back as she hauled him into her sweet, slick sex. From this position she couldn't do much more than slam him into her, which was the exact opposite of what he wanted. She wouldn't control this pace. She wouldn't rule his body as she'd already taken over his head, filling him with her so that he breathed her in every time their bodies merged.

If he went faster, if he yielded to the demands of his own longing, this would be over. A night that wasn't. A memory he refused to put on the shelf until he'd wrung it dry.

But his hips picked up the beat anyway, lunging into her while she opened herself to him and let him take. She massaged him from inside, her walls clasping him in a spasm that pulsated all the way from the head of his dick to the soles of his feet.

"Harder." She rocked into him, her head bouncing against his shoulder. Her pale breast bobbing like a buoy in the boiling ocean that surrounded them. "I want it."

His cock took up the charge without his help, surging into the searing clasp of her body in a ceaseless rhythm. He bruised her with his punishing hold, deliberately testing her limits, and she only grew more slippery and hot. Trying to corral her desire was like tossing a Molotov cocktail into a forest.

Once more he pulled back in a futile attempt to prolong the inevitable, but she gripped him deep and tight, ripping a shout from him when the first gush of her release took him under. Her orgasm rippled all the way through him, as strong as the lash of rain against his back and neck. He drove into her over and over, his climax firing pinwheels of light behind his closed lids. An explosion of white-hot energy, unleashed.

His breaths sawed in and out of his parted lips and he mumbled against her hair, breathing in its fragrant lavender scent before he gave into a moment of blissed-out exhaustion.

She trembled in his arms, around him. Reminding him they lolled against a door that could open at any time, on top of a public building.

A building he owned.

"Dillon?"

He cocked open one eye and blinked as it stayed dry. The rain had let up while they'd been plastered together. "Hmm?"

She shot him a grin over her shoulder. "So, was it good for you?"

He dropped a kiss on the tip of her nose. Probably not the usual gesture after rough door sex, but it fit. "Try spectacular."

"Did you see lightning?"

"Affirmative." He looked up and noted the clearing skies. A slice of moon peeked through the gap in the clouds and he couldn't stop the grin that crossed his face. "It even stopped raining."

"It was raining?"

Laughing, he pressed a rueful kiss to her shoulder and eased out of her. That she made a weak sound of protest went a long way to making him feel better about leaving the silken fist of her body. He wasn't the only one who hated to see this end.

Even if it never should've happened in the first place.

He pulled off the condom as she tugged up her shorts and bent to adjust her shoes. Or at least that's what he assumed until she turned and dangled the handle of his watering can from her fingertip. A sexy smile ghosted around her mouth, scarcely visible in the moonlight. "Aww, a daisy. Missing this?"

"It's a watering can," he muttered, snatching it out of her hand.

"I know. I've used them before. You know, a lot of men might be intimidated by using such a...cute item." Another sexy smile. Damn if he didn't find them delicious.

"If I didn't prove my manliness a few minutes ago, then screw the daisy."

She laughed and the sound smoothed away most of his ire. Unluckily for her, since he'd been half-tempted to "prove his manliness" by taking her against the stone railing.

"Need some help?" She had apparently noticed his full hands and pulled up his jeans and boxers for him, tucking him inside the cotton with an efficiency that got him half-hard all over again. "So did you really put this garden together?"

"It's not just a garden," he said through gritted teeth. "It's an ecologically viable green roof." Something he might've told her more about, had he not been much more consumed at the moment with the way her nipples beaded against her top. He could have it off and her breasts in his palms again before a moan passed her rosy lips.

"Is it part of some beautification deal? Or to save some cash?"

God, he needed to dump this condom and lose the watering can. Holding both somehow made his chest puff and his manhood shrink in disparate proportion.

He tossed the condom in the nearby garbage can and returned as Alexa was redoing her braid. Shit, he'd pulled it to pieces. "It's not just about money."

"Only rich people say that," she said under her breath, wrinkling her nose in a way he guessed was supposed to convey displeasure but instead made her look freaking adorable. "Are you trying to blend in with the moneyed set?"

"I've been trying for years." Definitely a true statement. "There are heating and cooling benefits for buildings with green roofs, yes, but they're also a good move for the environment and wildlife." He tucked the watering can under his arm and opened the door. "Come on. I have your part."

Falling silent, she followed him downstairs and up the hall to the apartment he'd been working on earlier that evening. He set aside what he'd been carrying and grabbed the bag he'd left by the door.

"I'll put it in now, if you want," he said, hating the awkwardness he could already sense building between them.

Sure, everything had been hunky-dory when they'd both been horny out of their minds, but now reality had arrived. They were near strangers, and worse, he was keeping something huge from her. Even if she hadn't wanted to hear the truth, that didn't diminish his guilt in holding it back.

"Where did you get that?" She stared at the part tucked under his forearm. *Fuck*. He'd forgotten to lose the bag.

It wasn't as if he hadn't tried to get the part in Renault, but the hardware store had been closed when he arrived. So he'd come back to Value Hardware just before closing and grabbed what he needed, thinking he'd ditch the evidence and she'd be none the wiser.

Yeah, not so much. Apparently that cheerful smiley face imprinted on plastic might as well have been the bell at the start of a boxing match. Any second she'd put up her dukes.

"Why do you hate Value Hardware so much?" Maybe, just maybe, he might even be able to come clean and not feel guilty as hell for digging through her financial records, then having dirty roof sex with her while she believed he was just the full-service handyman.

"Where do you want me to start?"

"At the beginning."

She huffed out a breath. "They don't care that they're squashing the little guy."

"You mean you," he said gently.

Irritation flared on her face and she threw her braid back over her shoulder. "Not just me," she said, crossing her arms across her chest. "They're trying to do everything instead of what they're good at. First they were just a hardware store. Now they're expanding into flowers and landscaping. I even heard talk in town they want to do some snooty lifestyle magazine. It's like they want to put everyone out of business in Haven but them."

If Dillon knew his brother—and he did—Cory wouldn't mind that. At all. "Diversification's good in this economy. Besides, you can't blame just one store if your business isn't doing well."

Unless there was more to it... and *unless* was a word practically made for his brother.

Her eyes flashed. Damn, but she was pretty when she was riled. Pretty all the time, prettier when she had a flush tingeing her skin and that fire in her eyes. "Oh, and you're an expert now?"

"I'm just saying there has to be more behind why you hate Value Hardware so much. You don't hate Zulo's, I bet, and they sell plants too." Or did she hate Zulo's? Hope bloomed in his chest. Perhaps she had an all-encompassing retail hate, which was a little creepy and yet also would let him off the hook.

His gaze lowered from her pursed lips to that dangling necklace flirting with the vee of her tank top. Her nipples pebbled under the thin ribbed fabric, making him stiffen against his jeans.

Then they could have sex again. Soon.

"No, I don't hate Zulo's. I reserve my hatred strictly for Value Hardware." She sighed and looked at her watch. "I should go. I have to be up early."

"Me too." He'd be talking to his brother first thing, because something still wasn't right with this whole situation. She'd just had an incredible orgasm—thank you very much—and yet she was already strung tight again at just the mention of the hardware store. He got that she was stressed about money, but he could tell there was more. There had to be.

If he couldn't figure out what the problem was, he couldn't fix it. And if he couldn't fix it, he couldn't get another hit of Alexa. And that wasn't an option.

"I'll be by soon to put in the part," he added into the silence. The air practically crackled with renewed sexual energy.

That he couldn't take advantage of again yet. Unfortunately.

"Thank you. I appreciate you fixing my sink earlier, and getting the part." She turned toward the door.

"You forgot to thank me for the orgasm," he called with a grin just before the door thudded shut.

• • •

Alexa scrubbed the counter inside Divine, determinedly buffing out every last fingerprint from the glass. It wasn't as if she had any customers to help. It was just past noon and she'd already been open for three hours. In that time, she'd had two browsers and two non-buyers. There had also been a visit from her brother, who'd stayed just long enough to ascertain she was once again without help in the store. Oh, and that she basically had no customers.

The good thing was that the lack of foot traffic meant she'd have plenty of time to work on her new window display that afternoon. She'd decided to take a page out of Value Hardware's book and do up some pretty, inexpensive displays with a fun fall theme. She glanced at the pile of paper flowers, wire, and swaths of bright red-and-yellow ribbon she'd bought at the craft store. Her inner snob wanted to sneer, but the rest of her was excited. It had been so long since she'd done arrangements that weren't high-end, pricey affairs with the most expensive flowers and exquisite silk bows. It would be fun to really let her creativity go.

Besides, what did she have to lose? Nothing she'd done so far had worked. She'd happily content herself playing with her carnations—what the hell—and loops of bells.

Speaking of bells, the one over the door chimed and she glanced up, her heart beating faster. Nope. Not a customer. Or…anyone else she might foolishly hope to see, though she knew she shouldn't.

"Hey, Travis," she said to the college kid who'd been helping design Divine's new website. "Get out of class early?"

"Yeah. Had an exam." Travis's sandy brows lifted toward his equally sandy thicket of unruly hair as he studied the gleaming counter. "Look at you go."

She shrugged. So she was a bit obsessive-compulsive when it came to keeping the store clean. There were worse things she could do.

Like sleeping with your new building's handyman after knowing him only one day?

Warmth suffused her cheeks. Yep, not going there. Though "sleeping with" seemed like a painfully inadequate term for what had occurred last night between her and Dillon.

Not that she knew how he felt about their sexcapade. She wasn't the insecure type to need progress reports from her lovers, but for some reason she'd been tempted to ask him last night beyond her cheeky "was it good for you" bit. Then they'd fought over plastic bags and Value Hardware and she'd flounced off instead of going for round two as any sane woman would have. The arousal in his hot blue eyes had indicated he'd been more than willing to play product tester on another vertical surface, but the mention of the store had killed her libido. Beyond stupid.

Now Value Hardware was even screwing with her sex life — and her sink.

She sprayed more glass cleaner and attacked a new spot. Just as well they'd argued. At least she could now say she'd driven Dillon away and wouldn't have to concern herself with wondering if he'd want more than a wham, bam, slam against the door.

On the roof. In the rain. With the stars just coming out in the rolling sky, while their wet, hot bodies rubbed against each other —

"Lex?"

Guiltily, she looked up at Travis's address. "Yes?"

"I asked if you needed anything before I got to work on the site." He gestured to the broom and dustpan tipped against the counter. "I could sweep up if you'd like."

He was a sweet kid. Always volunteering to do chores for her. "Thanks, but I have it all under control. I'll order out for lunch in a bit."

"I can man the store if you'd like to get some fresh air. Or I can run down to the deli and pick you up whatever you'd like." His eager smile coaxed out one of her own. "How about the usual? Pastrami on rye? Extra pickle on the side?"

"Such a sweetheart." She leaned forward and patted Travis's arm. "But thank you. I'll just finish up and go later."

The bell over the door dinged again and that same futile

hope reared in her chest. Stupid. She and Dillon had mutually agreed to have a one-night stand—half-hour stand?—and there was no reason to second-guess that decision. If she saw him around her building, fine. She would be cordial. But there would be no more sex. Absolutely none.

She tried not to groan as Nellie and her father entered the shop, beaming. "Afternoon, sweetpea." Her father came around to wrap her in a hug while Nellie clasped her hands and looked motherly. Not just because of the formidable baby bump, but she also had that anxious expression in her eyes that Alexa's mother often did. The one she hid behind abundant cheer, as Nellie was right now.

Uh-oh.

"What is it?" Alexa gripped her father's upper arms and peered over his shoulder at her best friend. "Is it the baby?"

"No, of course not." Nellie patted her belly as if to reassure herself it hadn't detached and rolled away. "We're just here for a visit. We brought lunch," she added, holding up a brown paper sack.

Double uh-oh, and now that uh-oh was directed *her* way. She recognized the looks on their faces. If they weren't keyed up over the baby—thank God—someone else had set off their worry button. And that someone clearly was her.

Just great.

"I can take a short break. Hang on." She went to the back room and aimed a grim smile at Travis, who was kicked back at her desk with her MacBook Air propped on his knees. "Just going to borrow these," she said, snagging the two spare folding chairs.

He immediately sat up and tried to look serious. "Need help?"

"I've got it."

"Okay. I'll get back to work then."

Did he really think she hadn't noticed the game window he'd minimized as soon as she appeared? But he was a good kid and what he'd done so far on the site looked amazing. She wouldn't begrudge him a couple minutes chasing birds or whatever he'd been doing. "You do that."

Once the seating was arranged around the counter and sandwiches were open on everyone's laps, Alexa decided to go for broke. "Since when are you two hanging out together in the middle of the workday?"

"Since Jake had a meeting and your mom was stuck in court and I needed a ride to the ob-gyn," Nellie replied, pulling off the crust on her ham salad sandwich.

"A, I'm your best friend, why didn't you call me? And B, what's up with your car?"

"In the shop. Broken axle. Besides, you're working and Pop told me I could ask him for anything."

Alexa almost choked on her tuna on rye. "Pop?"

Nellie grinned. "Yes, what Jake calls him. He said you refuse to call him anything but Father."

"Too true," her father put in, busily inhaling his own turkey and Swiss.

"Not true. I call him Daddy sometimes."

"Yeah, when you want something. Like when you begged and begged for that Miata for two years in high school."

"And you gave it to me for graduation." Alexa smiled fondly at the memory of her first car, a pristine white convertible. It hadn't had a single dent when she'd sold it four years later after college.

"Your first love," Nellie agreed.

Alexa's smile faded. Did they really need to talk about love? She didn't want to think about anything that had to do with men. Not when she was battling serious second thoughts about cutting-and-running when it came to Dillon. Even if it could get messy with him working in her building. Even if he had purchased a part from Value Hardware, which really wasn't a crime at all. It was just that she'd still been suffering the sting of Patty's defection, and he'd waved that smiley-faced bag around…

"I don't need anything," she said under her breath, fiddling with her sandwich. "Everything is just hunky-damn-dory."

Her father took a swig from his soda, then set the bottle aside with a finality that made her nervous. Here it came. The real reason for their impromptu visit. "Sweetpea, there's nothing wrong with asking for help from people who love you. Who only want the best for you."

"I don't need help." Hadn't she just said that?

Her father and Nellie exchanged knowing glances. "We disagree."

"Oh, really." She glanced back and forth between them, not liking this united front they were presenting against her. Nellie was supposed to be her best friend. On her side in all things. Even those that had yet to be discussed. "Help with what?"

"Well, let's start with the sign in the window."

"The sign that's been there all of two hours?" Alexa rolled her eyes. Suddenly it all made sense. Her caped crusader of a brother had blown his bugle and spread her news all over town. "Jake called you, didn't he?"

"He might've mentioned he stopped by here this morning, yes." Her father didn't blink. For a guy who worked in accounting, he had a steely *don't argue with me* stare. "What happened to your new employee? Didn't you just hire her?"

Alexa fiddled with the wax paper that held her mostly uneaten sandwich. Her appetite was about as consistent as her emotional landscape lately. "She found a new position at Value Hardware." Nope, the words didn't singe her tongue.

At all.

"So you need someone to help you," her father prompted.

"Well, yes, I'm hoping to find someone. Preferably with flower design experience, but I'm willing to train the right person." What else did she have to do during all the hours she *wasn't* helping customers? "I'll even take part-time at this point, assuming they can start within the next couple weeks."

"Perfect." Nellie balled up the wax paper that no longer contained her sandwich. Apparently she'd put it away already. "I just resigned from Gamble's this morning. I'm a free woman."

Alexa gaped at her best friend. Nellie had worked at Gamble's for years, and despite getting fed up with the gossip mill, Alexa had thought she liked her job. Plus there was the employee discount, which allowed her to feed her cheesy shirt fetish on the cheap. "You quit the department store? With no notice?"

"I offered to work two more weeks, but Mr. Gamble turned me down." She shrugged. "Honestly, I've been ready to leave for awhile. The politics just got to be too much, and I'm tired of listening to sniping. Besides, you said the magic words. Part-time." She grinned. "So when would you like me to start?"

Chapter Four

When considering all the ways he could be spending a sunny day, willingly entering the icy domain of Cory Berkeley Santangelo was not one Dillon would've picked. Especially considering he was reasonably certain his brother was up to something. He had to be.

But that his brother was in the midst of a knock-down, drag-out fight with a petite blonde sporting chopsticks in her hair mitigated his displeasure.

"Victoria, we have company." Cory's jaw was tight enough to dislodge his teeth as he marched around his desk and resumed the seat of command, effectively dismissing his nemesis and the interior designer helping to stage VH's lifestyle magazine, Vicky Townsend.

That they'd been sniping at each other for most of their lives should've lessened some of Dillon's enjoyment, but he'd only been back in town a few months. He'd missed their combative style of foreplay, though Cory would've flipped had he known Dillon saw it as such.

"Dill, it's so good to see you." Vicky rushed across the room to hug Dillon. "I heard you were back in town, but you must've been hiding out."

Dillon returned the gesture and grinned at Cory's glower as he turned to his computer. Keys clacked with the impatience Cory couldn't have hidden if he wanted to. "Been busy. You know how it is." He held Vicky at arm's length and tweaked her chopsticks. "You look hot, Vickster. Making all the boys beg, huh?"

"Except you." With a wide smile, she slugged him lightly in the stomach and glanced over her shoulder. "And the master of gloom and doom," she muttered, making Dillon laugh.

"I'll speak to you later. I have business to discuss with my brother." Cory's impervious tone made Vicky and Dillon grin at each other.

"Ooh, I'll just make myself disappear then, since you have important *business* and all." Vicky stepped back to gather her large coffee-table books and fat portfolio. She leaned in close to Dillon on her way out. "Help him take the stick out of his ass, would you?"

"Hell no. He's on his own."

Vicky's trill of laughter followed her out. When Dillon turned to Cory, he still hadn't wiped the grin off his face. Vicky had always been the perfect partner in crime—and the ideal thorn to jab in Cory's side.

"What did she say about me?" Cory demanded.

"Something about sticks and your ass. Which you're on your own with, dude."

Cory scowled and leaned back in his captain's chair. As usual, he was dressed impeccably. Today he wore a navy suit, crisp white linen shirt, and precisely knotted yellow tie. "To what do I owe this surprise visit?"

"It's not such a surprise." Okay, so it was.

"How is the Kelly apartment looking?"

"It's coming along." Though his brother hadn't invited him

to sit, Dillon dropped into the chair opposite Cory's massive oak desk and threw an arm over the back. Cory usually raised a brow whenever he sat like that, as if he anticipated a visit by the formal office police. "I'll finish installing the new living room flooring by tomorrow. The kitchen floor's next, after I deal with the AC. It's not getting cold enough in some of the apartments so there may be a leak."

"Is that really necessary? The AC work is one thing, but new floors?" Cue the raised eyebrow. "I was in there several weeks ago. The tile didn't look that bad."

"It's a mess," Dillon said flatly. "If you want to attract decent tenants, you have to do the up-front work to make sure they'll be happy."

"That unit is already rented," Cory reminded him, his tone clipped.

"I realize that. I also realize some of the other units could've used that attention to detail *before* rental agreements were signed."

Cory's gray eyes turned as cold as sleet. He didn't appreciate his judgment being questioned, something Dillon had been doing since, oh, birth. "Which ones?"

"Mrs. Fairleigh's been calling all week saying there's a leak above her balcony."

"That leak has been fixed."

"Apparently not, since she claims it's still dripping."

"You're the one who's made it clear that you want to limit your participation in the business to manual labor. You've had ample opportunities to do otherwise, yet you insist on throwing up drywall and promoting charity balls." Cory flipped a pen through his fingers, evidence he was still rattled from Vicky's visit. Score one for the interior designer, since it usually took extreme provocation to throw him off his game. "You know this can't last forever, this save-the-earth thing you have going. Dad wants to move. Once they do, they'll be out of the business. It'll be you and me."

"I'm here, aren't I?" Dillon asked, unable to keep the testiness out of his voice. He knew all of this. He'd known it yesterday on his long bike ride, and he'd known it last night when he'd had the most amazing sex of his life with Alexa. That should've never happened, but damn if he could bring himself to regret it.

"Being here's not all there is to it. I need you to be a full partner with me, Dill."

It had been a long time since Cory had sounded so…well, sincere. No smirk. No glare. For once, he seemed genuine.

"I know," Dillon said quietly. "You can count on me."

Their eyes locked for a moment before Cory nodded. "You've been adamant about wanting to handle the bulk of the renos on the buildings, since your name's on the properties. So if things aren't up to snuff, isn't it your job to fix them?"

And just like that, they were back into their roles. Cory as the big businessman, Dillon as the day laborer and secret do-gooder, whom Cory turned to when he needed his spreadsheets to balance correctly.

"There's also Ms. Conroy's unit. She had a sink issue yesterday that needed to be fixed, and considering it was her first day in the new apartment, she was understandably unhappy. There are also problems with the drywall in the bathroom, along with some missing grout in the shower stall."

"I would suggest yet again that you don your Superman cape and get over there and fix it, but that would just be redundant, now wouldn't it?" Cory waved a hand at the scrolling numbers on his sleek, ginormous flat-screen monitor. "Now if you don't mind, I have — "

"How much are you charging her?" Dillon interrupted.

"Lex?"

"Ms. Conroy," Dillon said, surprised by how vehemently he didn't like his brother referring to her with such familiarity. Especially when that familiarity came with a leering lip curl that didn't seem kosher for a man threatening to evict her. "How much rent are you charging?"

Cory swiveled to his keyboard and tapped a few buttons. "Nine-fifty."

Dillon clenched his jaw. "Are you frigging serious? For a studio?" Narrowly he resisted adding the rest on the tip of his tongue: *And you wonder why she's behind on the rent for her store?*

"It's a competitive rate. Next year when we've finished rehabbing the rest of the units and completed remodeling our other buildings, Alexa will realize she's gotten a deal. Haven is a town poised for huge population growth fueled by Synder Corp.'s expansion. It's only a matter of time."

Dillon fought not to roll his eyes. "You sound like you're running for Common Council."

"Yeah, well, you sound as if you want to flip out a grass mat and start chanting." Cory tapped more keys. "The rate's even been locked in for her protection against inflation. What may seem high now will end up being low as the local economy improves."

"Mighty big of you."

Briskly, Cory brushed lint off the arm of his jacket. The master of the universe didn't like being questioned. "You think I'm a hard-ass?"

"Rhetorical much?"

"I didn't even have to rent to her, Dill. Most other people wouldn't have, since she's a known credit risk with her business. Divine Flowers is her store," he added when Dillon didn't reply. "The previous owner, Rosalind Keller, was constantly behind on her rent too, but I realize that's not

Alexa's doing. Apparently Lex has been trying to dig her way out since Rosalind's death. I'm sympathetic to her plight, but sympathy can only go so far."

Again with the *Lex* stuff. "So you've met her in person then."

"She's been here to plead her case more than once. I invited her to dinner some time ago." The last bit was said distractedly, as if Cory wasn't fully aware of what he was saying.

Dillon tightened his fingers into a fist. "How'd that work out for you?"

"She turned me down." A brief smile crossed Cory's normally unsmiling mouth. "Quite unapologetically. I think she believed I was behaving unprofessionally."

Way to go, Lex.

"Weren't you?" Dillon asked, his irritation diminishing. They hadn't gone out. Silly to be concerned about something that had obviously occurred way before he'd been back in town.

"All I had in mind was a friendly dinner. What's with all the questions about Alexa?" He shook his head. "I know what this is about. Dad told you about Taste of Froot."

"What's Taste of Froot?" Dillon stretched out his long legs in front of him. "And what does it have to do with Alexa?"

"Taste of Froot is a high-end, specialty line of dessert shops. There are two stores in southern New York and the owner would like to build one in Pennsylvania. Naturally, Haven is on her short list for locations."

"Naturally." As the dots connected in Dillon's head, his temple throbbed. Alexa's anger suddenly made a lot more sense. And sense was what he needed to talk into his brother before he did something he couldn't take back. "Wait a second. You want Alexa's shop for this fro-yo bar?"

"It's not merely fro-yo." Cory steepled his fingers together. "And yes, if you must know, Divine Flowers' current location would be perfect for Taste of Froot. It's centrally located on Main Street, near the shopping district. Not to mention, Alexa is delinquent. I'm sorry, but it's true."

Talk about kicking a woman when she was down. Shove Alexa out, stick in a trippy yogurt place. They owned other property. It wasn't as if the yogurt shop couldn't slide into another opening. In fact, they owned an empty storefront on the other side of Main, yet another of the projects Dillon had on his slate for the fall. Though that was probably the problem. The empty storefront needed work. Alexa's store was in move-in condition.

Since the bulk of their ancillary properties were in Dillon's name as per the agreement he'd made with Cory, he'd willingly agreed to handle rehabbing them. Eventually he would end up managing them as well. In the meantime, Cory was handling things.

Which meant, in effect, if Alexa were evicted, it would be by Dillon, not Cory. For all Dillon knew, Cory had been signing his name to the letters of warning all along.

Man, his brother was a piece of work.

"So you're courting her?" Dillon asked, tightening his jaw around the question.

"Courting who?"

Interesting. "The chick who owns the dessert places. Oh, wait a second." A sly grin crossed Dillon's face. "Do you know her? Like…personally?"

Cory raked a hand through his previously undisturbed dark hair. The nervous tic didn't suit him, but his glare sure did. "Of course I know her personally, as we're fostering what I hope will become a mutually profitable business relationship."

"No, I mean *personally* personally." Dillon grinned. The subject of women was one they could discuss without too much rancor, assuming Cory stayed away from Alexa. "Is she hot?"

"You're a complete Neanderthal."

"That's a yes. So tell me about her."

"There's nothing to tell. Yes, she's attractive, just as she's always been. Can we move on?"

"As she's always been, hmm?" Dillon stretched his arms behind his head, quite liking holding Cory's feet to the fire. Too bad he didn't get to do it more often. "So who is she?"

Cory shoved back from his desk, though he didn't rise. His hair slipped forward, flirting with eyes that had narrowed. "Melinda Townsend."

Metal Mindy? "Vicky's older sister Mindy? No fucking way."

"*Melinda*," Cory enunciated. "She doesn't go by Mindy anymore. She's an incredibly successful businesswoman and we'd be lucky to land her store in one of our properties."

"Aw, look at you getting all fidgety. How cute. Is that why you're cozying up to Vickster? Trying to get in good with the sister?" Though that was a lost cause, as far as Dillon could tell. Vicky and Cory had been like a lit match and polyester for as long as Dill could remember. That Cory had never quite shaken his infatuation with the gorgeous, untouchable Met— Melinda—had never seemed to sit well with Vicky either. Sibling rivalry or something, probably.

Not that he knew anything about that.

"I'm not cozying up with Victoria. How could I? She's an ice cube."

A laugh burst out of Dillon. "Vick? Are you kidding me?"

Cory's features eased. Marginally. "Just so you know, I didn't contact Victoria. She came after me. Once word spread that we were considering doing a lifestyle magazine to augment the business, she practically begged me to hear her spiel. So far all she's done is argue with my choices."

"She's a very well-respected designer. Nationally acclaimed even."

Cory's mouth flattened. "It's my magazine. She's completely inflexible. And irritating as hell."

Dillon leaned forward and rested his arms on his thighs. This was absolutely priceless. "So, did you ask her out yet?"

"Excuse me?" Cory choked out.

"Melinda," Dillon said, not getting why Cory seemed to be having trouble breathing. Then he realized his brother hadn't quite caught on to his topic shift and barked out a laugh. "Jesus, you thought I meant Vicky? Hell no. She'd kill you in a day."

"Maybe I'd kill her." Cory turned back to his computer. "It's not appropriate for me to ask Melinda out," he added.

"You asked Alexa."

"You're obsessed with Lex." Cory eyed him with speculation. "Are you obsessed with Lex?"

"Alexa," Dillon corrected, ignoring the question. "But you wanna ask Mindy out. Desperately."

"I have work to do. Go hammer something."

Dillon chuckled and rose. He might not have figured out how to stop Cory from trying to evict Alexa or how to improve Alexa's rent situation, but he'd gained some valuable fodder to use against his brother. One thing at a time.

Besides, maybe he could figure out how to help Alexa all on his own without involving his brother. And without her being any the wiser.

Yeah, probably not, though that didn't mean he didn't intend to try. Giving up—especially now that he knew what she was up against—wasn't in his vocabulary.

"Good luck with Meta—"

"Get out of here," Cory interrupted with a grin just before Dillon shut the door behind him.

. . .

"Have a nice day!" Alexa called to the customer on her way out the door, barely smothering a sigh. Yet another non-buyer.

August was often a slow time unless a shop booked a lot of wedding-related events. Not that she had the staff for that. She'd set up a booking for a "farewell to summer" party two weeks from now, but she knew that was mainly due to her father being friends with the client. Besides, it was a small event, twelve tables with small arrangements on each. She and Nellie could do those in a day.

One day she hoped she'd be able to do bigger, grander events. Her new splashy website was part one of that plan.

"Hey, Trav, come out here for a minute, please," she called. "Bring the computer."

He trotted out obediently, the Mac under his arm. "Yeah, Lex?"

"Can I see how far you've gotten on the site? I'm hoping to roll it out sooner rather than later."

"Sure." Travis set the computer up on the counter then brought up the site, pointing out a few of the features. She liked the colors they'd decided on, cream and maroon, which tied in tastefully to the colors of the shop. Roz had always fought Alexa when she'd mentioned developing a web presence, but Alexa hoped she would be proud of how Alexa was doing in her stead anyway.

The numbers weren't there yet, true. All that meant was that she'd have to work harder—and smarter.

"I just set up Divine's PayPal account this morning, and

I'm hoping to have the other pages finished by the end of the week. You know, for upcoming holidays." He frowned and clicked on the Fall Inspirations page. "You have a ton more pictures of Halloween displays than anything else. The fall page is super crowded."

She shrugged and smiled at the photo of a huge wall wreath made out of real autumn leaves and interwoven with thin strips of orange and black silk ribbons. Fat sunflowers curved along the bottom. The special-order piece had taken hours and was still one of her favorites. "So I love Halloween. Sue me."

He glanced over his shoulder, his lips pursed. "Do you still get dressed up?"

"If I have a reason to." Laughing, she poked him lightly in the shoulder. "If you're asking me if I don a witch costume just to sit home and watch monster movies, no. I don't."

"Too bad." A grin lit up his face. He started to respond, but yet again, the bell jingled.

This time when she glanced at the doorway, a broad frame filled it, almost blocking the sunlight with his shoulders.

Dillon.

Joy came first, followed by her usual pragmatism. He'd probably just come to tell her he needed to get into her apartment to work on her sink.

"Hello," she said, suddenly very aware of how she'd been draped over Travis's shoulder while she peered at the computer. "How may I help you?"

Dillon's gaze landed on Travis first, though the kid had already grabbed the computer and started backing away. "Hey," he said to the younger man.

"Hi. Call me if you need me, Lex." Travis spun on his Nikes and disappeared into the back office.

Alexa almost called him back, then decided maybe it was

better to deal with her handyman one-on-one.

Dillon's eyes narrowed, as if he was trying to decide what he'd seen. "Friend of yours?" he asked, sauntering farther into her store.

He seemed so huge among the glass and chrome tables of flowers. Capable of destroying delicate blooms with a gust of breath. But when he gingerly cupped a lilac tulip bulb in one of his large palms and directed a raised eyebrow her way, she realized his tender touch made up for his size. And how.

"Employee." She kept her tone cool. "Travis is my web designer."

"Redoing your site?"

"Doing it for the first time, period." She resisted fiddling with her cup of maroon pens, emblazoned with the store's signature script logo. "Divine's previous owner wasn't eager to embrace the digital age."

"Me neither. Always did prefer a pen and paper to e-mail. It's so impersonal."

He strode around the perimeter of the shop, looking at everything. Occasionally he stopped to touch an arrangement or to consider a display of Chilean jasmine or frangipani, but he remained silent.

She watched him survey her store and bit off a slew of impatient questions. It didn't seem natural for Dillon to remain so quiet. Okay, so she didn't know him well enough to gauge that, but she considered herself a good judge of character. He was acting weird. Where were his flirtatious comments, his hot looks? Even when she caught him examining a spot of chipped paint in one corner that probably no one else had ever even noticed—except her—his face remained impassive.

His spooky silence felt disapproving, though that was probably just her nerves. Still, would it kill him to say something? "Nice plant" would suffice.

She slipped off one of her pumps and scratched the back of her right calf with her left foot. Then she did the same with the other. Still nothing from Dillon.

Finally he completed his loop of the premises. "I like your place," he said simply.

She let out a relieved breath. He was probably just being pleasant. A workman-type guy like him most likely didn't care about flowers, though he did seem to take an active role in caring for the roof garden. But he smiled while he praised her store, and that was enough for her.

"Thank you."

"You seem to stock a lot of high-end product." He touched the yellow petals of a Hypericum, then moved on to study a pineapple lily crowned with its usual tuft of leaves. "Not many carnations or gerbera daisies in here," he said thoughtfully. "You know, like the painted ones?"

She bit the inside of her cheek. "I don't carry painted flowers. Divine has always sought to stock a wide variety of blooms, from all over the world. Carnations can be bought at any gas station." No need to mention the ones she'd ordered just that morning for her fall designs.

He moved on to study something she called a Zen garden, with river canes of bamboo, purple mokara orchids, and sword fern. Drawing a fingertip over the highly polished bamboo box, he cocked his head. "How much is this?"

"Seventy-three fifty," she said, fighting not to say more. When she was nervous, anything was liable to come out of her mouth. Most of it wasn't pleasant.

Dillon whistled. "Steep. The bamboo's nice, though. You carry ornamentals here?"

She couldn't figure out if she was pissed he thought her prices were high, amazed he recognized bamboo, or dazed that he seemed interested in the first place. "A few. They're grouped together in front of the window."

"Everything's in its place. All very organized."

"Shouldn't it be?"

"I don't know. Sometimes mixing it up can be more fun. Add to the sense that a person could find anything here, if they searched enough." He crouched to study the ornamentals, making the occasional "tsk" and "hmm." "I'll take this one," he said, picking up a small lemon tree in a heavy, ornate pot she'd shoved into the corner by the door. He didn't struggle under its weight at all, and even managed to pick up a rabbit's tail ornamental grass in a long, narrow box. "This too. Do you take special orders?"

His ease with the heavy plants robbed her of her breath, and made her blink at him as if he'd just crash-landed in her shop from Mars. "Yes. What do you need?"

"Sedum, in particular." He set the plants on the counter. "Do you have a catalog?"

His brisk tone snapped her back into business mode. "I have this," she said, reaching for a brochure. "I'll also have an online catalog as part of the site. There will be a section devoted to a wide range of plants, and their uses in home decorating in particular." Was he decorating his home? How did he know about sedum?

Then she remembered the roof garden and her skin prickled with heat, the brochure she'd grabbed fluttering to the counter.

And not because she was thinking about his lovely collection of stonecrops.

Apparently oblivious to her sexcapade hot flash, he leaned forward and picked up the brochure she'd dropped. "Nice," he said distantly, his expression hard to read. As usual. "Lots of Japanese flowers and pricey arrangements though. Not very accessible," he said, glancing around as if deep in thought.

"To whom?" Deliberately, she edged her voice in ice. "This is a specialty floral shop."

"Yeah, but it's empty."

She winced before she could school her response. "Right now, yes, but—"

"And where are your doodads?" he asked, studying her counter and its neat stack of business cards and cup of pens. "And a sign-up sheet for your mailing list?"

"What mailing list? What doodads?" She knew which way she was heading now. Straight into *back the heck off, buddy*.

"You know how stores place trinket-type crap near the checkouts to get people to impulse buy? You need that here." He dragged his fingertips over her previously pristine glass counter, ensuring her another session with the Windex before the end of the day. "Something cute and cheap. Like, I don't know, small arrangements. Or even flower-themed stuff." He snapped his fingers. "What about those little climbing creatures that go on flower pots? Squirrels and stuff."

Alexa linked her fingers together on the edge of the counter and took a cleansing breath. He was a potential customer and her building's handyman to boot, so she couldn't kill him, no matter the provocation. "I'd ask you to list all these fine ideas and stuff them in the suggestion box, but oops, don't have one. So let's move on, okay?"

He didn't appear to hear her. Now he was studying her ceiling, of all things. "This place is too sterile. How do you feel about chimes? Or those wind spinner things? With the baubles on the end that blow in the breeze?" Then he glanced at her sharply. "And you need an e-mail list at the very least. Get a clipboard out on the counter, start gathering names. I'll be your first."

Rarely-acknowledged violent impulses reared up inside

her, and only sheer force of will kept her standing still. She plastered a thin smile on her face. "Let me get the website up and running before I tackle newsletter lists, mmkay?"

To her endless annoyance, he didn't seem to notice her response to his bullheaded suggestions. With a tilt of his head, he regarded the pen-and-ink drawing of a daisy on the wall. "Pretty. Local artist?"

"Yes. My mother."

"She's very talented."

"Thanks." Idly, she rubbed a vague ache in the pit of her stomach. Nerves. Something about Dillon set her off-kilter. Well, lots of things did, but now that he'd stopped peppering her with ideas about her business, she was referring to his sharp-as-a-tack eyes. Or his killer smile. Or his sizzle-hot body, which she knew way too much about, and wished she could learn more.

He slanted her a glance. "Do you draw? Or paint?"

"God, no. I can barely write legibly, never mind doodle a picture." She laughed, then fell silent when she noticed how closely he was looking at her. At once, her traitorous body reacted at the memory of what they'd shared.

So much for being mad at his high-handedness.

Her nipples tightened, and her panties flashed damp. Any time now he'd leave and she could go back to fantasizing about how he'd felt inside her while she stewed over his obnoxious know-it-all attitude. "What are you doing here, Dillon?" she asked, more softly than she'd intended.

He waved a hand at the items he'd placed on the counter. "Along with these plants, I need some flowers."

Disappointment came first, swift and humbling. Clearly he hadn't been magnetized to her store by his need to ravish her beside the ornamentals. "Oh."

A smile tipped up his mouth. "I bet you thought I was

going to bug you about getting in to fix your sink."

She toyed with her necklace, well aware that his gaze dropped to her breasts every time she did so. "Maybe. You seem like a dutiful type."

He chuckled, low and deep in his throat. "Still think that after last night?"

Don't blush. She wasn't one to get red and stammer by nature, but this guy had a way of making her feel like a girl in the throes of her first crush. Or perhaps first sex thrall. "A woman never kisses and tells. But yes," she worked her chain between her fingers and pulled lightly, "I still think you're conscious of your responsibilities. Look at all the stuff you're buying for the roof garden. Your employer will be pleased."

Something dark flashed through his eyes, moving as quickly as a summer squall. Then it was gone.

He crossed his arms over her counter, bringing her attention to the flex of his forearm muscles. Damn, he was hot. And he made *her* hot, inspiring an anticipation inside her she hadn't felt in way too long. She couldn't wait to see what he'd do next.

"Speaking of pleasure…" She swallowed hard as he trailed off. "I know you'll get an immense amount of it knowing your sink is fully operational, so I'm going to fix your pipes this afternoon, Alexa." His sexy voice caressed her name as if she were naked in his arms. "Beyond that, just say the word."

He was talking pipes for pity's sake, and she was burning up like a locomotive chugging oil. Her chest hurt from her rapid, suppressed breaths. God, if she didn't watch herself, she'd toss off her clothes, mount the counter, and beg him to fuck her. And that just wasn't part of the plan. A quickie sex romp on the roof was bad enough. A repeat would make meetings in her apartment building even more awkward. Not to mention she didn't have the time or mental space for any sort of relationship right now, even of the screw-and-rue variety. She needed to focus on making Divine a success, and she didn't need his advice on that score either.

Everything was under control. *Her* control.

"Fine." She didn't elaborate.

He nodded, his disappointment evident in his open blue gaze. "About the flowers. I normally buy from—"

"Don't say it." She held up a hand. If he'd come to her for flowers, she'd help him find a small, affordable bouquet even if she had to throw something together on the fly. She glanced at the lemon tree and rabbit's tail. Though cost didn't seem to be a huge factor for him. "You have your plants. What type of flowers were you looking for?"

"She likes roses."

All she heard was she. *She* who? But her professional smile never faltered. "What sort of relationship is it?"

"Excuse me?"

"Different colors of roses signify different things." To help distract herself, she strode to the glass-fronted cool case that held an impressive rainbow of roses. She had a fondness for them too, though her preference ran to the rarer—and therefore more expensive—varieties.

"Oh yeah?" His eyebrow ring winked in the sunlight as he gave her his full attention. "Like what?"

"Well, red typically means love." He better not pick red, unless he wanted to endanger certain vital parts of his manhood. "White stands for purity of intention. Coral can mean desire, and purple..." She fell silent.

"What about purple?"

She cleared her throat and narrowed her eyes hard on the display so she couldn't see him out of the corner of her vision. "Purple means love at first sight."

He didn't reply for so long that she chanced a glance his

way, only to discover he was smiling. "Purple's your favorite color. You must have a romantic soul."

The sound she made in her throat embarrassed her, but not as much as the flush creeping across her cheeks yet again. "This was just some poetic type's idea of how to sell flowers." She hurriedly stepped behind the counter. "It's not reality."

"Who's to say what is reality?"

She rolled her eyes. "You're not one of those types, are you?"

Dillon prowled to the counter and leaned in, just close enough that she could smell the foresty scent of his aftershave. Or his soap.

An unexpected image of him rubbing a mint-green bar over the hard planes of his body formed in her head and her mouth went dry. Damn. It looked as though she'd be spending some quality time with madame butterfly tonight, since her rooftop sex-o-rama hadn't taken the edge off. Or maybe it had honed a whole new one.

"What sort of type would that be, Lex?"

She jolted from his usage of her nickname. "Call me Alexa."

"Why? Too personal?" His smile spread as he traveled his gaze down her form. "When we've already gotten so personal already…"

"Shh." She cast a quick look over her shoulder and sent up a prayer that Travis hadn't abandoned his post in the back office.

"Afraid your friend will hear?"

"Employee."

"He doesn't look at you like you're his boss." Considering, he scratched his smooth jaw. "Then again, maybe I'd be similarly starry-eyed if any of my bosses had looked like you when I was in college and full of—"

"Let's just stop right there." She didn't want to think of Travis as full of anything. The boy was barely twenty, for God's sake.

"Fair enough," he agreed with a chuckle. "So about those flowers."

"In a hurry to get back to work?" she asked pleasantly. *In a hurry to buy roses for your anonymous* she?

"Not in a hurry, but yeah, I've got some stuff going this afternoon beyond your bathroom work. I figured I'd ask since I know you have privacy issues and all."

"I do not have 'privacy issues.' I just wondered if you were as conscientious and all-knowing with everyone."

"I make it a point to know as much as possible," he said, tone sober.

"Ass," she muttered, tossing a pen at him.

He laughed and stuck the pen in the breast pocket of his denim work shirt. A work shirt he'd just rolled up even farther, revealing his sinewy forearms and dusting of light brown hair. Not that she'd noticed. "I'll be out of your place by the time you get home."

"Do you know what time that is too?"

His lips quirked. "The sign says you close at five. I took an educated guess."

"Hmph." She fiddled with her three-part forms. "You said bathroom work, which sounds like more than fixing the sink. What else do you need to do?"

"Just some patch-up plaster work. I apologize for the state of the apartment. I should've been more thorough before it was rented out."

"Well, it's not like you own the place." She laughed off his concern. "You just do what you're told, right?"

"Most of the time." He reached out and danced his fingertips over the back of her hand so fast that she didn't have time to prepare for the move. As if she could. Heat slammed into her and she opened her mouth to draw in air. Or gasp. "I wouldn't mind taking orders from you," he added in a placid tone that warred with the suggestiveness of his molten gaze.

"Which roses did you want?" she asked a little breathlessly.

He pursed his bitable mouth while he considered. "Think we'll go with red."

Frowning, she noted the appropriate box. Red. Of course. "A dozen?"

"Let's go with two. Hell, make it three, with lots of the green stuff." He jerked his chin at the arrangement of stuffed bears climbing up the potted vine behind her. "Stick in a few balloons and one of those teddy bears, would you?"

Chapter Five

Alexa's surprised expression clued him in to his mistake.

Shit. Three dozen roses wouldn't be cheap. It hadn't occurred to him to worry about price. Why should he? He could've bought out the whole shop—hell, bought the store itself—though that would've been a little ridiculous considering he already owned half of the building. Technically.

Dillon glanced around the store. A place that meant so much to her belonged partially to him. He couldn't decide if that made him feel good. Right now it was just weird.

"Three? Are you sure? And the bears are thirty dollars."

"Maybe we'll skip the bear," he said in an undertone, feeling foolish.

Dammit, he'd wanted the bear. His gram would've loved it. But a thirty-dollar bear and three dozen roses would be a prime invitation for Alexa to indulge her suspicious nature. Life had gotten so much harder since the invention of the internet.

It was probably a miracle she hadn't done some checking up on him already, in light of her stalking concerns. Though those probably weren't too serious if she'd reacted to him the way she had when he'd stroked her hand. The jolt that went through her still thrummed through him, as well.

Touching Alexa was way too enticing. Because if he wasn't careful, touching would lead to holding, and holding would lead to kissing, then he'd be pulling her back in his arms again. Maybe bending her over this counter and—

"Okay. No bear. Would you like to select a card?" She spun the card carousel. "They're free," she added.

"Oh, what a relief."

Jeez, even pretending to have a strict budget was depressing. His mood had plummeted in the last two minutes and all he'd lost was a bit more of his integrity.

Yet more proof he needed to come clean.

Great sex or not, bottom line, he never should've slept with her. Even if she'd said she didn't care who he was, she hadn't realized what she was saying. It wasn't right to not come clean, and he'd also likely screwed up whatever slim chance existed that she might want to see him outside of bed. Or hell, even inside of bed again.

He wasn't his brother, dammit. The idea of evicting a longtime small-business owner to take an offer from someone who wanted to put in a fro-yo place didn't get him all atwitter. At least he'd discovered that Cory wasn't completely a heartless ass when it came to Alexa's situation. But the conversation with his sibling hadn't given him a solution, assuming he considered Alexa's financial difficulties his dilemma to solve.

Did he?

What he wanted, more than anything, was to be there when she figured out how to make her store a success. She had a great shop and obviously she possessed a lot of talent. Her heart showed up in her eyes whenever she spoke about the place. All she needed was a little time, a little luck, and a little help. Something he could give her—but only if he didn't come clean just yet. If he did, she'd paint him with the same brush as his brother and discount everything he said. Worse, she might assume he was trying to sabotage the store.

He couldn't let her risk her business that way, not when he was certain she could—*they* could—make it work. And if her success goaded Cory, so much the better. His brother claimed he enjoyed competition, didn't he?

After the store was on its feet again, he'd tell her the truth. Maybe she'd even be grateful he'd fought his own instincts to reveal all to help her. Yeah, so maybe not, but at least she'd have her store, whole and strong and in the black.

And he would have her, if only for a short time. Perhaps he'd even rediscover his own love for business by working on something that wasn't Value Hardware. Something smaller, and more personal.

She looked up at him with her glossy blue eyes and his stomach flipped over. Whether his plan was good or not, it didn't even feel like he had a choice in the matter anymore. He was pretty damn invested, both with Alexa and with her store. Bystanders didn't suffer a spike in blood pressure the way he just had simply from a look.

"Did you want a card? You're not looking at them." Her cross expression shouldn't have made him hard. Nor should've her disturbingly erotic fragrance, especially in light of where he was. Floral scents surrounded him, yet he could pick out Alexa's unique perfume without hesitation.

Man, he was in trouble.

"I'm looking at you." How could he look anywhere else?

He expected her to sneer at his cocky declaration, and she did just as he'd hoped. "Think a lot of yourself, don't you, Mr. James?"

"Just stating the facts, ma'am."

Her pupils dilated, leaving just a fiery ring of blue to highlight the dark. "You never said who the flowers were for. A crush, perhaps?"

He fought not to grin at her obvious irritation. *Jealous much?* "As a rule, Ms. Conroy, I don't get crushes. When I want someone, I go after them. At all costs." She didn't need to know how long it had been since he'd felt that way. It was both humbling and a little disturbing. "Even when I know I shouldn't."

"Maybe that's part of the appeal."

Holding her gaze, he ran his tongue along his lower lip. She mirrored the gesture, though he was sure it was unconscious. "I'm a contrary bastard. Knowing someone wants to put me off only makes me want them more."

"So it's just the thrill of the chase to you."

As her hand strayed to that damn necklace, he let his stare sear her flesh. The subtle tightening of her top across her breasts proved the look worked. A little too well, since his jeans had gone tight too. Painfully so.

"A chase is only as good as the prize." He cocked his head as her breath quickened. "I like to work for it."

Lust flared in her eyes before her veil of curly lashes swept down to hide his view. "Dillon, we agreed it would only be one night. You know this can't happen again."

Keep trying to convince yourself, darlin'.

"It already is." As Travis ambled into the shop, Dillon slipped back and flashed her a smile. "I'll take the bear. I think my grandmother will like it."

• • •

Alexa came home that night to a perfectly functioning sink and a clutch of pink-and-white mountain laurel in a mason jar on the windowsill, but no sign of Dillon. She didn't even notice the flowers at first in her haste to search for signs he'd been there. He'd left nothing behind, not even a stray boot print.

But he had left her the laurel.

She couldn't help sighing at the sight of it, limply leaning against the glass rim. Simple or not, the gesture was sweet. So sweet that she refilled the water glass and added half an aspirin in the futile hope of staving off the flowers' demise a little longer.

They were obviously handpicked, which made them even more precious to her. Imagining Dillon's big hands picking through them, searching for just the right blooms...

She sighed again. God, the man must be a frigging expert archer, because he'd just nailed her square in the heart.

The next night when she returned home to the smell of fresh paint, she found another bunch of laurel, this time with a note.

Sorry I didn't ask before stopping in, but there are some things that need taking care of around here. If you want a rundown of what, or if you'd like to yell at me for invading your privacy—and insulting your sense of aesthetics with my pathetic flowers—my number is 201-8801. D.

The smile came before she could stop it. Holding the note to her chest, she followed the paint scent to the bathroom. He'd painted two walls a cheery lake blue. Patches of white decorated the third wall as if he'd done some prep work to finish tomorrow.

She could smell him, a hint of his pine aftershave and soap. If she drew deeply, maybe the slight tang of his sweat, layering lightly over the rest. It had been a hot day, and the small window he'd forgotten to shut didn't offer much breeze. The inadequate AC would suck this summer, though oddly enough it seemed to be working better now.

Her smile widened. But she had new flowers.

Not giving herself time to squelch the impulse, she ripped off a piece of the notepaper he'd found on her end table and scrawled a quick reply.

I like the color you picked for the bathroom. It reminds me of Gillie Lake on a clear day. And the flowers are so pretty. Thank you. You're welcome to do whatever you'd like to the apartment, without my permission. A.

The next night she returned home to a fully painted bathroom, a half-moon daisy rug in front of the sink—an exact match to the watering can she'd laughed at him for toting around—and a new mason jar of flowers on the windowsill. She blushed as she took in the bluish-purple blossoms. Forget-me-nots. Too bad he didn't realize how truly fitting they were.

Best of all, there was another note. Grinning, she snatched it up.

I'm glad you liked the paint. You don't have to keep the rug I bought, but when I saw that daisy at the thrift shop today, it reminded me of you. Everything seems to lately. D.

Her belly fluttered just imagining him in her apartment, filling it with his scent while she worked downstairs in her shop. While she stared out the window in the hopes of glimpsing him on his way into the building and fought the persistent daydreams about him her brain insisted on conjuring up with disturbing regularity. Of him making her feel alive in a place that didn't seem nearly so depressing when he was at her side.

His hard, muscled body knew just how to move against hers to wipe away everything but him. She had no worries, nothing to fear when she and Dillon were together. It was just them. God, all that heat and passion and need—

"Stop," she whispered, shutting her eyes.

She'd said she wanted one night. How could she change

her mind so easily? She didn't know him well, but they probably couldn't be more different.

But she knew one sure way they were compatible, no questions asked.

She pulled off another piece of notepaper.

Thank you. The rug made me smile, just like the flowers. I like that you're thinking of me. I'm thinking of…well, nothing that has to do with you and flowers, but maybe I wouldn't mind seeing your snake. A.

The next evening, Alexa came home to a gray and dreary apartment. The drizzly weather definitely hadn't helped her mood. She'd had a blah day with not one, but two snarly customers, and only one of them had purchased an arrangement.

She sighed and set aside her purse on the table inside the door. Only one bright spot cheered up her gloom—maybe Dillon had left her another present. Or better yet, perhaps she would find him stretched out naked on her air bed, ready to do her bidding.

A girl could hope.

But alas, there was no Dillon in her apartment. And no flowers. Tonight a plastic snake peeked out of the jar on her windowsill.

Laughter spilled out of her as she grabbed the note he'd left behind.

When you said snake, I got confused. If this isn't what you had in mind, call me. I'm all done working on your apartment. Let me know if you need anything else. D.

She added the note to her secret stash at the bottom of her kitchen drawer and filled up the forget-me-nots' jar of water, along with adding a new crushed half-aspirin. She did the same with the jars of mountain laurel on her small kitchen table. The makeshift vases were in a triangle, the drooping flowers making a sad sort of statement. But she refused to throw them out.

How long had it been since a man had brought her flowers? Or a cheerful daisy rug she couldn't help grinning down at as she brushed her teeth? Never, that's when.

He'd fixed her sink, and freshened up her bathroom, and touched up the paint along the living room baseboards. Even better, she realized as she stowed her raincoat in the empty closet by the front door, he'd given that a thorough paint-and-clean job as well.

Dillon James had figured out the way to her heart, and it was pathetically simple. Though she'd spent the last year denying she needed anyone but herself, right now, she just wanted someone to take care of her.

At work, she was in charge, and she had to be strong. She couldn't let anyone see her break, though sometimes she found herself fighting tears as she put together arrangements she knew she'd have to take to the hospital and local cemetery before the week was through. Not that she didn't like doing her part to cheer up others. But the flowers she replaced on graves every week weren't all that was dying. Her mentor's beloved business was, as well.

She wanted to call Dillon so badly that her fingers twitched, but she couldn't offer much to anyone right now. An uncomplicated relationship she could handle. Something with a definite beginning and end. The possibility of seeing Dillon any time she was at home or work made this potentially a lot more messy. She couldn't handle any more potential messes, not when the sense of impending failure consumed her night and day.

No matter what she did—whether it was starting new advertising campaigns or arranging huge, showy bouquets of blooms in the front windows of Divine—the customers just weren't interested. She hadn't given up. Not even close. But tonight the breakwall around her emotions felt on the verge of collapse.

It wasn't as if the news was all bad. She schmoozed every customer she managed to lure into the store, offering them amazing service and a plethora of complimentary add-ons. Her special attention to every person who entered her shop would hopefully bear fruit in the form of repeat business in the years to come. Especially once she started that e-mail newsletter list she couldn't deny was a damn good idea.

But in the meantime, she was floundering.

"Not me," she murmured, staring into the nearly empty closet she still hadn't closed. She'd yet to unpack most of her suitcases. "The store. Not one and the same." Even if they felt damn close.

When her stomach started to growl, she got up with the intention of scrounging for dinner. On her way to the kitchen she grabbed the pile of mail she'd brought up with her from the store. Today it contained mostly magazines and the occasional bill, but nothing she couldn't handle.

Until she reached the legal-sized envelope from Santangelo, LLC she knew was yet another overdue rent notice. Soon they'd stop saying "if you don't, we will" and just set a date for her to have to get the hell out of the store.

Tears spurted into her eyes and she shook them off. *No.* She was not going to cry. Her plan to save the store was going to work. She just needed a little more time.

Giving in to the urge to wallow, she sat down on the floor and drew her legs up to her chest. And rocked.

She wasn't down for the count. Nellie had started working with her yesterday, and she'd begun showing her the basics. They'd worked on fall wreaths that afternoon, twisting colorful ribbons into bows, winding delicate blooms and vines through grapevines and around wire frames. Her best friend seemed to have a natural eye, thank God. They'd laughed and laughed as they worked, something Alexa hadn't realized how much she'd missed.

Losing Patty was a big blow, but with Nellie's help, Divine would be okay. It wasn't as if there was a ton to do right now anyway, except the usual orders and inventory and keeping everything tidy. She just needed to keep the faith and not let this temporary black hole suck her in.

After a while, she rose unsteadily to her feet and called Trixie. She gave her cat her daily dose of love and kibble, then sat down on the couch and turned on the TV. She smiled. Dillon had taken it off the dinky stand she had for it and mounted it at the perfect height on the wall without her even having to ask.

Between Dillon and Nellie, kindness seemed to be spilling out all around her lately. Perhaps it was a sign her streak of bad luck was finally going to end. Maybe she needed to go see Sue Ellen, Nellie's tarot-reading cousin. She could use some guidance. Along with another night with a certain man, who happened to have a sexy grin and incredibly athletic hips.

Ah, screw it. What did she have to lose? Except everything?

Biting her lip, she dialed Dillon's number. Silly to be nervous. He was just a guy, and she knew how to handle men. Usually. Somehow her typical moves hadn't resulted in the dance she'd expected this time.

He didn't answer, so she left him a voice mail. Though she attempted to sound breezy and casual, she was sure she failed. There was that word again. *Failure.*

The night passed in a haze of junk food and sitcoms. She sat through a couple reruns of *The Big Bang Theory* and noshed on Twizzlers, since she'd yet to fill her pantry with anything substantial. Halfway through the nightly news, her cell buzzed in her lap. She'd just forgotten to put it back in her purse. It wasn't as if she'd been waiting all night to hear the sound of Dillon's voice.

"Alexa?" he murmured once she answered. "Are you okay?"

Oh God. That question, said in such a painfully understanding tone. The already weakening walls in her chest cracked open so fast she had no hope of shoring them up again before a sob escaped.

She couldn't answer. All that came out were broken gasps as she scrambled to hold back the deluge intent on spurting out of her eyes.

"What is it? What happened?"

He sounded frantic. As if he actually cared. Why should he? He didn't know her beyond a night of sex—truly incredible sex—and a note-and-flower flirtation. If she needed help, she had no right to expect it from him, when all she had done was dismiss him in her mind as "just a handyman."

Which was total crap. He wasn't just anything. There was nothing wrong with being a handyman. It was an honest profession, and she was too bitter and tied up over her own nonsense to even give people a fair shake anymore.

Kind of like the fair shake you refuse to give yourself?

"It's just been a shitty day. Nothing unusual there," she laughed bitterly and pressed her fingers to her closed eyes, "until I got the mail and another overdue rent notice. Nothing new there either." So why was she on the verge of tears again just from telling him?

"I'm coming over," he said, his voice harder than she'd expected.

"It's okay, you don't have to. I'm all—" She couldn't even get out the protest. How could she, when all she wanted was to spend more time with him?

For a while, she needed to get away from her own brain. Whatever it took. Still, she wasn't sure if a guy she barely knew qualified as a good person to let herself go with. Mindless sex was one thing. But what if she couldn't stop the tears and he saw her in her current state of soggy mess? Did she really want to go there?

"I'll be there in twenty minutes," he said. Then he released a huff of breath. "Have you eaten?"

She glanced at the candy that had served as her dinner. "Not exactly."

"I'll get us something. Anything you hate?"

"Sushi," she replied, feeling steamrolled but in the best way possible.

"No sushi, got it. See you soon."

Alexa clicked off and forced herself to straighten up. There wasn't much mess to begin with, but tidying gave her something to do.

At the last minute she remembered Dillon's flowers. Gotta hide those. No mush allowed. She tucked the jars behind the gauzy white curtains that framed the lone kitchen window. The struggling violet she'd babied all week took the place of honor in the middle.

It took more time to straighten herself up. Her eyes were red and puffy, her cheeks blotchy. Fabulous. He'd be riveted by the sight of her tonight.

She raced through a cool shower and threw on the boy shorts and eyelet-trimmed cami she slept in. Then she eyed herself in the mirror. Hmm, maybe she should go with a strapless bra for a little extra support. While she debated the point, she fiddled with her wet hair, finally tossing it on top of her head in a clip.

The knock on the door answered her bra question

succinctly enough, though she was ridiculously conscious of the slight sway of her breasts as she hurried to answer. From the quick glance at her chest Dillon tried to disguise, he'd obviously noticed her lack of mammary support.

She'd noticed something else—namely the aroma of hot Chinese food coming from the bags he carried. Her nose practically wiggled with interest.

Yeah, she was flashing him a message, all right. *Do me. But feed me first.*

"Alexa?" Warily, he reached out to tip up her chin. After a careful study of her eyes, he nodded and pushed the bags into her hands. "You look hungry."

"Do I?" She supposed that was better than looking weepy. Getting ready for him had given her a welcome task to focus on. Her forgotten stomach growled as she waved him inside. "Everything smells great."

"It's nothing fancy. Just some Chinese."

She swept her gaze from his stubbled jaw to the dusty toes of his boots. As usual, her attention caught first on his gleaming eyebrow ring, then the bright blaze of his eyes. His brawny shoulders stretched his thin, yellow T-shirt until the fabric wept, and his muscular torso led to lean hips encased in low-slung jeans.

No doubt about it, the guy was sexy. Though she still wouldn't have called him classically handsome, his looks were growing on her.

Like ivy. Or fungus.

"Chinese is my favorite, especially from that little place on Whelden." She noticed the logo on the paper bags and grinned. "Excellent choice."

"I love them too. Best egg rolls ever." He dug in one of the bags and pulled out a sleeve bulging with egg roll contraband. "Three of these are mine, but you can have one."

"Gee, thanks." It made her laugh, but the brief kiss he smoothed over her temple quieted her once again. "I appreciate your interrupting your night for me, even if it wasn't necessary."

"Says who? I missed you." Her heart turned over as if he'd flipped it in a skillet. "And I was having so much fun, I can't even tell you. What a huge interruption." Amusement filled his tone.

"Why? What were you doing?"

"Tearing off a roof, then when it started to pour, I attacked some drywall. Literally. Wasn't too careful, hence the blisters and calluses." He flipped over his hands and showed her his palms. "Well, more than usual."

She glanced down at his wide, blunt-tipped fingers and remembered them on her body. *Inside* her body.

A tingling flush swept over her face. What was it about this guy? She couldn't seem to suppress her hot flashes around him. Nor could she kill the sex thoughts. Really dirty and creative sex thoughts, preferably involving honey or whipped cream or maybe even duck sauce. Hey, necessity was the mother of invention and all that.

"Alexa?"

She did a mental double take at her veer into no-man's land. "Yeah, sorry. I'm distracted tonight."

He smiled crookedly. "I have a feeling you weren't thinking about shingles."

"No?" she asked, all innocence. "Why ever would you think that?"

He let his gaze drift down to her top. Specifically, what was *under* her top. "Your nipples are hard. Before you say it's chilly, it's not. It's humid as hell." He pulled out the neck of his T-shirt. "I'm sweltering."

It took all her self-control not to suggest he strip. Quickly.

In the interest of his health. "You're right. Fair warning. I'm in a strange mood. As you heard on the phone." She swallowed over the knot in her throat. "Sort of swinging from lust to despair and back again. I'm not really sure if I'm interested in talking or sex, or both."

"But are you in the mood for Chinese?"

She returned his smile. If anything, it had widened. "Absolutely."

"Then we'll take the rest as it comes." He rested his hands on her shoulders to guide her toward the kitchen. The lump in her throat eased even as other parts of her grew tighter and wetter. "Just don't eat my egg rolls." He brushed a kiss over the shell of her ear.

She gave into a delicious shiver. The Dillon special, she was discovering. "Your egg rolls are safe." She threw him a teasing glance over her shoulder. "But as for the rest of you, no guarantees."

He grinned. "Let's eat fast, flower girl."

Chapter Six

They dawdled over dinner, Dillon's earlier *eat fast* directive soon lost in a lazy, meandering conversation that greatly resembled one of his motorcycle rides. Usually he didn't pick a route, just chose each road as he came to it. Veering right, then left, then right again, following the slant of the sun or the shadows the leaves made over asphalt. Sundays were his to while away as he wished, alone on a back road. That was his heaven on earth.

Spending time with Alexa Conroy was another.

The pain he glimpsed in her eyes called to him, coaxing a gentleness from him he hadn't given in to often enough. He liked taking care of people—and yes, women in particular, as rare as it was for him to get that involved with one these days—but somewhere along the way, he'd stopped doing it other than in his work with the charity and with his family. On a personal level, it was much trickier business. But Christ, he didn't want to turn into Cory, so isolated and caught up in his work.

Lately he'd become too obsessed with the manual aspects of his job that wore him out and left him little time to dwell on the future, when he'd always loved getting out there and talking to people. He didn't need to become a Cory clone. Hell, his mother had flat-out said they didn't expect that. There were all sorts of possibilities for him to further embrace his role in the business.

Such as helping a store renting one of his properties.

If Alexa succeeded, so would Value Hardware. They could work together. One business feeding the other. Fuck, he didn't even like frozen yogurt.

"You're being too nice," she said, sipping her take-out cup of coffee.

The raspberry chocolate blend wasn't his favorite, but he'd had a feeling she would enjoy it. He'd been right, as proven by her delighted squeal after he'd gone down to the car to grab the forgotten cups. "Is there such a thing?"

"When you've spent as much time as I have trying to show everyone that you don't need help then yeah, there is. I've already let you do so much for me and I haven't put my foot down." She smiled. "Or thrown a hissy fit."

"Yeah, you did. Remember your reaction to where I got the part?"

"Trust me, that was me set on mild."

"You? I don't believe it." Actually he did, quite well. She was fire and ice, sweet and a hell of a lot of spice. Especially in that little cotton ensemble she had on now, with its lacy straps, delicate pink-and-yellow flowers, and high-cut shorts that showed off her endless legs.

His dick had hurt since he'd walked in the damn door. Shit, just glimpsing the shadows between her breasts made his thoughts dive right for the gutter. Never mind her hard nipples, outlined in vixen-innocent cotton. What he'd give to suck them while he sank his fingers inside her again. And this time he wouldn't stop until he'd tasted all of her.

"I'm Daddy's little girl. Mommy's too." She sighed as if she'd just shared a weighty secret. "For most of my life, I took whatever was offered me, because hey, it was my due. All hail the princess." She toasted him with her cup, obviously remembering his name for her.

With a few notable exceptions, she'd dropped the princess routine so swiftly he half-wondered if he'd imagined it. Then they'd come together that night, and learned a lot about each other awfully fast. Her walls had come down, and some hadn't fully come back up. Yet.

He was scared how much he wanted to keep her open and bare to him. *For* him. Not to exploit, but so he could find the real Alexa. Though he'd yet to share the real Dillon James with her, the one with a financial empire he'd yet to fully lay claim to, but would have to soon.

Working with the Helping Hands charity and rehabbing the business's income properties had actually eased him back into the fold faster than he'd expected. Earlier today his stepfather had asked him to do a demo in the store next week of a new line of miniature power tools, and he'd not only agreed, he was looking forward to it.

Slowly but surely, he was moving into the role he'd been meant for all along. With his parents' impending move, the time had come for him to step forward. Maybe he'd even find a use for his office yet—besides having a place for his freelance charity organizer to work when she needed a stationary location—especially considering his timing couldn't be worse with Alexa. He might as well enjoy his temporary sex life now, since the more steps he took toward Value Hardware, the further he moved from Alexa.

Even if she didn't realize it yet.

"Why'd you change?" he asked, wishing he could erase her pensive expression.

"I wish I could say I had some big lightbulb moment, but it was more insidious. I suspected Roz was sick." She pressed her fingers hard into the sides of her coffee cup. "She never said a word. I complain if I break a nail, but she was dying and she never felt sorry for herself, not for one minute. So I tried to keep up a brave face for her while she was still running the business, but I started checking into the books. And I saw how much trouble we were in."

"She died last year."

"Yes. She was young. Too young. It took a while, but looking back, it was all so quick. There's never enough time." She blew out a breath. "Nellie and Jake were falling in love at the same time. My brother and my best friend," she explained. "And Roz was just gone. She'd been my babysitter growing up, one of those family friends who sort of drifted away, but our bond never changed. She was as close to me as my mother. In all the ways that mattered, she was my mother, right along with my own."

He shifted on his chair. "How do you find so much room for people inside you? You already had a mother."

Much to his relief, she didn't stare at him as if he'd just revealed a forked tongue. "I love my mom to pieces, but we've always had a weird relationship. She doesn't fully get me. Neither does my father. Jake is their golden child. The one who pleases them by breathing. I'm the one they have to watch."

"Why?"

"It started when I was caught skipping school in junior high and sort of devolved from there." She shrugged jerkily and drank more coffee. "I'd skip class and go shopping. Date all the bad boys and miss curfew. I think they half-expected me to either get expelled or end up pregnant by senior year."

"Neither happened?"

"No." A grim smile curved her mouth. "I don't mess around with birth control, and if I commit to doing something, I do it. No matter what. Skipping school occasionally didn't mean I didn't care about my grades. Trying cigarettes and maybe even something a little stronger," she coughed delicately, "at a party was just about having fun."

"Until Roz died." When she nodded and drained her coffee, he passed his across the table. "Here. More your speed than mine."

"Don't like coffee?"

"Don't like girly coffee," he corrected, enjoying her eye roll and quick smile. Alexa not smiling seemed like a world injustice somehow. Seeing her amused, even only for a moment, went miles toward restoring his own balance.

"If you insist." She took a long sip, her eyes meeting his over the top of the cup. "Though with all this caffeine, I'll be up all night."

He toyed with the wire around one of the Chinese food cartons while he worked on maintaining his casual slouch. Even if every nerve ending in his body perked up at the possibilities. "Ms. Conroy, are you propositioning me?"

"If I was?"

"I'd say hell yes and get naked."

Her husky laughter made him grin. "Everything seems so much easier when you're around. I don't know why. It's like I can think again. The weight of my life doesn't strangle me when you're sitting across my dinky table."

"I'm glad." He gripped her free hand, running his thumb up and down between her knuckles. "What's strangling you, Alexa?"

She didn't answer at first. Her lashes swept down to block her eyes then she glanced up and looked at him directly. "I think I'm going to lose Roz's business." She let out a broken laugh. "Actually, no. Not lose it. I think I'm killing it, one exotic flower at a time. I can't make it grow. Bills are piling up, and every day it just seems more futile. No one wants what I'm selling."

"I'm sure that's not true. You do incredible work, and you have a beautiful store."

"You really think so?"

Finally, some hope. He clung to that thin reed in her tone and nodded fiercely, determined to help her rekindle that inner fire he'd seen only a few days ago. Where had it gone? Buried under overdue bills, most likely. "Yes. I know so. Your flower quality is incredible and you have designs in your store I haven't seen anywhere else."

"No one cares about that. All they want is cheap. Ask Value Hardware."

The name nearly jolted him. He slid his fingers down to clasp her wrist, noting the rapid beat of her pulse. "What are you doing to drum up business?"

In a halting voice, she told him about ad campaigns and flyers and special sales. About ideas she'd had for classes, and the new website she was having built. Throughout, she held herself in a stiff position, as if she didn't really believe what she was saying. As if the business was already dead.

"Don't give up." He tightened his hold on her wrist when she didn't look at him. "Do you hear me, Alexa? You're doing this to honor your friend, your second mom. You haven't come this far just to turn around and tuck your tail between your legs now. Just hang on a little longer."

"For what? What exactly am I waiting for, Dillon?"

"For your faith to pay off." He rubbed his thumb in absent circles over her palm. "You're all you've got, and you need to fucking fight for all you're worth."

"And if I fail, it'll hurt just that much more."

"You'll only fail if you stop. If you can't trust yourself anymore, trust me when I say I know you're going to be fine. You're not going to lose your business."

She swallowed hard. "What are you afraid to lose?"

A handful of glib answers sprung to mind, but he remained silent. If he couldn't tell her who he truly was, at least he could cut the BS and give her something real.

"Myself," he said softly. "I may not be the best guy in the world. God knows I have my flaws. I was always so damn stubborn about doing everything on my own. But sometimes, you really figure out who you are as part of a team." He looked up and found her studying him. "Sometimes you gotta commit to seeing something through, shoulder-to-shoulder with the people you care about."

As the words left him, he realized how true they were. Not just about him and his family, but about Alexa as well. He wanted so badly to help her. To make her store work, and in turn, show Cory that not everything could be resolved on a profit-and-loss ledger. There were people involved. It wasn't all just about making money, but making connections.

Except he'd lied and pretended to be someone else to the one person he felt he could really be himself with—if he didn't happen to share a bloodline with Cory Santangelo.

If he told her the truth now, he'd risk driving her into the hole he sensed she was on the edge of falling into. What good would it do to make her question herself more when she realized she'd been had—and by the handyman, no less? Not that he'd ever meant to deceive her for malicious reasons, but she wouldn't believe that. She'd see his sudden arrival in her life as one more shiny nail into the coffin of Roz's legacy.

He couldn't do it to her. Or himself.

The only thing he could do was fully commit to the path he'd set. As angry as he was at Cory for causing her more pain with his damn notices, he knew kicking his brother's ass wasn't the way to handle this. She needed to get the store back on her feet herself if her self-esteem was going to survive the blows of the past few months.

And he would help her any way she would let him, for as long as it lasted.

When she murmured, "Stay with me," he couldn't walk away. If this was all they could be to each other, then he would savor every moment. And bide his time while he figured out a way to help her pull the rabbit out of the hat at her shop.

Maybe then she'd want him to stick around for longer than a night.

"There's nowhere else I'd rather be," he said as she came around the table and folded herself into his arms.

• • •

Alexa expected sex. More, she expected peel-the-paint-off-the-walls and call-the-cops-from-the-noise lovemaking.

What she got was a black-and-white movie and Dillon's hard chest serving as her cushion as they tangled together on her sofa. It wasn't a bad trade-off, all things considered.

He toyed with her hair throughout the movie, and the soothing motions of his hand relaxed her more than she'd been in forever. Even his muscled body cradling hers wasn't enough stimulation to keep her eyes open. Twice she jerked awake, and each time he nudged her back down with a soft "Sleep" that acted as an instant sedative.

The third time she woke, he didn't nudge her back down, just smiled at her in the glow from the TV and finger-combed her snarled curls away from her face. "Hey, sleepyhead. Feel better?"

"Much." She gave in to the urge to wrap her arms around

his torso and snuggled in. He smelled so good, like minty soap and sawdust, and the combination had her softening against him. She'd never been a cuddler, but right then she couldn't resist. "Thank you for staying."

"It was a good movie. Two good movies," he amended with a laugh as she poked him in the ribs.

"Who says chivalry's dead?" She shifted and barely repressed a smile at the definite hardness between his legs. She moved again and he let out a soft protest, not even hiding his interest. "Feels like some parts of you didn't get much rest," she teased.

"With you on top of me? That would be a no."

His almost resigned tone made her laugh. She leaned up to press a kiss to the underside of his chin, delighting in the prickle from his growth of beard. "I want to see your tattoos. If you're good, maybe I'll show you mine."

He drew back to regard her with curiosity. "You have one?"

"Mm-hmm." Playing coy, she lowered her lashes. "I do."

"Hmm." He slipped his hand under her cotton top, his palm resting lightly on the small of her back. "I bet it's right here," he added, tracing the line of her spine.

She shivered from his feather-light touch. "Nope."

"No?" He toyed with the shoulder strap of her cami, his eyes dark in the light from the TV. Utterly focused on her. "Let me see."

"If you insist." She fumbled for the remote and turned off the TV before straddling his waist. On the verge of pulling her top over her head, she startled when he laid his hand on her belly.

"Hang on. Let me up."

She sat back on her haunches and watched him unfold that long, sexy frame in one slow motion. He flicked on her newly purchased box fan—though the AC seemed to be working better now, she still got hot at night—then yanked on the sill of one of the windows. "It's fucking hot in here," he muttered, grunting as he lifted it.

A draft of humid, rain-laden air wafted over her and she shivered again at the tightening in her nipples. Though it wasn't just the breeze that made them wake right up. Those broad shoulders, silhouetted in moonlight, had a lot to do with it too.

He moved to the other window and shouldered that one open as well, finally returning to her while the faint bluesy notes of a saxophone bled into the room.

"Jazz club on the corner," he said, correctly reading her questioning expression. "Well, it's just a bar normally, but they have weekly jazz nights."

"Oh. I like it." She cocked her head as he stopped beside the couch and flicked on the small Tiffany lamp. "The sax is sexy."

"So's light, and seeing all of you."

She didn't respond, since he'd reached back to tug his T-shirt over his head. Hot damn, he had the kind of abdomen a sculptor could spend a lifetime trying to get just right. The contours of muscle and bone, the dusting of hair that arrowed into a happy trail down his stomach, the small black outline of a skull-and-crossbones just above his left hip.

"Nice tat," she said, with an incline of her chin. "For a pirate."

A smile lurked around his lips. Combined with that faint cleft in his chin, she was in big trouble. "Hey, at sixteen, I thought it was badass." He flicked the button on his jeans and her amusement fled.

She wanted him naked. On her. In her. Filling her up.

In no time, he'd removed his boots, socks, and jeans. She

examined him openly, not shy about noting details while she gripped the cushions beside her thighs. His lean, cut hips drew her attention the longest, until she sucked in a breath and veered lower to his navy boxer briefs and the colorful snake tattoo peeking out under the band around his left thigh.

The laugh spilled out of her, though she cupped a hand over her mouth to try to hold it in. "Very…colorful."

"Thanks. My friend Jerry owns a shop, and I was his test subject. The wings on my arm were first. The skull next. After he did the snake, I said enough was enough. Last thing he did was pierce my eyebrow."

He hooked his thumbs in his boxers and dragged them down his muscular legs. Then she wasn't looking at his tattoos anymore, but somewhere decidedly more personal. His cock was firm and full and crowned with a dab of wetness she yearned to taste.

With the fan streaming warm air over her back and the subtle notes of the saxophone drifting through the window, the whole moment felt surreal. Any time now she'd wake up alone on her air mattress with her hand caught between her legs, the victim of yet another cruel wet dream. She'd had way too many this week. And now he was here in the flesh, and she couldn't seem to drag enough air into her lungs to compensate for the way he made her ache.

The sticky summer air had already added a fine mist of perspiration on her skin. She rubbed her hand down her throat. "Very hot."

He grazed her jaw with his fingertips. "I have to agree," he said, his stare lingering on her face before traveling determinedly downward, causing a swell of sensation between her legs. She was throbbing for him already.

"I meant you. The piercing especially." She rose onto her knees to caress the copper ring, then let her hand wander up to his scalp. His short-short hair made her palm tingle and she whimpered when he nibbled her inner arm. Tenderly. His warm, wet lips on her skin prodded her to the flashpoint in an instant, and an answering surge of arousal dampened her inner thighs.

"I want to see yours."

"My piercing?" Playfully she unclipped her hair. "On my earlobes?"

"Do you have any others?"

"Like where? Navel? Nipples?" His eyes slitted and she tilted her head. "Clit maybe?"

"You don't have any of those," he gritted out.

"No. But never say never."

"Right now I'll settle for these beautiful earlobes." He manipulated the diamond stud she wore, somehow nudging her closer to the edge with just the brush of his callused fingertip. "I intend to suck on them for a while. Before I suck on the rest of you."

His smoky, provocative voice rose above the music filling her head. The beat had changed into something more sexual and primitive. Its bass line pounded inside her, pulling her into a subtle sway she didn't fight.

Her fingers itched to wander over his body, to explore every nook and cranny. "I like your body." Boldly, she lifted her eyes to his. "I want you."

"Almost as much as I want you." He spread her arms to her sides and drew her up until they were standing together, her fully clothed, him fully undressed. She was still moving to the music, letting the rhythm carry her, and he soon picked it up, his hips subtly rocking into hers. Slowly. The ache in her center spread, tendrils of lust creeping outward until her body quaked.

"I love that you dance so easily. You did on the roof too.

Just shimmied a little, enough to make me crazy."

"I have music in my soul." Though she'd said it to make him grin, she didn't check to see if he did. She had a whole new preoccupation and it was way below his face.

She looked down at the swollen length trapped between them and wetted her lips. He must've read the intention in her gaze because he chuckled and possessively palmed her ass in her clingy boy shorts, keeping her upright when she would've gone to her knees.

"Your tattoo," he said against her temple. "Give me a hint."

She turned to face away from him, wanting to prolong their teasing as long as possible. The long, anticipatory slide into sex was her favorite part. The other night they'd gone at each other like animals, but tonight was different. From the sax music, to their languorous movements, to the longing that flowed like honey between them, this was all about easing into seduction. And savoring every second.

"Any guesses where it might be?" she asked huskily.

He linked his arms around her waist and nuzzled her hair, his cock leaving a solid imprint on her ass. "Your shoulder blade?"

"Try again."

His mouth settled on the back of her neck and he branded her skin with blazing hot kisses. "Your hip?" His hand trailed a path from one hip bone to the other, making a lengthy pit stop on her mound in between. Taunting her with the placement of his fingers. So close, but so far. He rocked into her again, picking up the thread of the new song that reverberated through the floorboards. "Your ass?"

She laughed. "No."

"Your thigh? Your stomach? God, your inner arm?" He touched every part of her as he named it, his growing impatience—and growing erection—making her want to giggle. And squirm.

"No, no, and no."

"Seriously?" All playfulness gone, he whirled her around in his hold and stared at her as if she had to be lying. "What the hell size is this thing? A postage stamp?" Then he grinned triumphantly and reached for her hair. "I know. The back of your neck."

"Nope." She took pity on him and stepped back to draw her cami over her head. She tossed it aside and let her arms fall, more than a little dazed herself by the look of awe that crossed his features. "It's a forget-me-not. The color's a little off. Mine's a bit more purple than the actual flowers. Normally they're a medium blue."

"Oh Christ." With reverent fingers he sketched the tattoo along the curve of her breast. "Damn."

She had to laugh. "Are you okay?"

"You've been hiding this under your clothes, and I had no idea." The rawness of his voice coupled with the overwhelming desire in his dark blue eyes set off a wicked pulse in her core. "It was too dark for me to see anything the other night, and the color is so light… I thought it was something tiny, in some discreet, usual place."

"No."

"Fuck, Alexa." Then his mouth was on her, his teeth pulling on the nipple while she cried out and cupped his head in hands that shook. He drew harder and she watched him, unable to tear her focus away. The bite of pain sent a bolt of excitement through her, and she gasped at the heat coursing through her lower belly. He licked his way around the tattoo, his eyes flicking up to hers as he lapped at the petals that encircled the hardened peak. "You taste so good. I want more. You gonna give it to me?"

She barely had time to comprehend what he was saying before he lifted her up as if she were as light as one of her ornamental trees and set her down on the wide arm of the couch. He tugged off her shorts and threw them aside, driving one hand up the center of her torso to hold her still while he brought his lips down between her legs.

"Dillon!" Her cry stunned her, because she couldn't have stopped the sound if she tried. He didn't give her a chance to catch up to his intentions, just left her clinging to her buttery leather sofa with one hand and his prickly scalp with the other. She fumbled to hold on as he slanted his mouth over her and gave her the most erotic French kiss of her life. "Don't stop."

He didn't answer, and apparently he didn't need to breathe either. He just latched onto her sex and used his tongue to drive her out of her mind, sweeping up and down as quick as a brushfire. Never landing anywhere long enough to truly make her burn, just igniting a million little sparks along the way. She arched against him, her need spiraling higher with each swipe. And then he circled in on her clit, sucking hard, and she raked her nails down the back of his neck in warning.

It was too soon, too fast. She wanted to take that ride with him. But he just kept on, laving her tight knot of nerves with short, focused strokes that increased the throb in her blood. The music built, the sax somehow getting louder, the floorboards beneath her tensed feet seeming to pound with its sexual thrum.

And she built too, until he slipped two thick fingers into her and she crested, coming up off the sofa with her cries spilling from her throat. She could only see him kneeling between her thighs, one hand on his cock, stroking, while he extended her pleasure until it straddled the edge of pain.

When he finally stood, she couldn't speak. She just watched him don a condom through hazed eyes, her hands idly cupping her swollen breasts. Adding more fuel to the aftershocks still spiraling through her system.

He noted the gesture with a growl as he bent to run the tip of his tongue down her throat, pulling a gasp from her as he nudged aside one of her hands and reclaimed her nipple as if it belonged to him. Right then she would've given him anything before he even asked.

He lifted her thigh, notching it on his hip and moving between her legs. "I like you like this. So soft and warm." She might've swooned had she not been partially reclining already. He rested his hand on her mound and toyed with her sensitive clit with his thumb. "And wet. You're so wet for me, aren't you?"

Once again he didn't give her time to answer before holding her leg wide and feeding his cock into her entrance. His girth stretched her sodden flesh, arousing her nerve endings all over again with his patient thrusts. He took his time sinking deep, then held her there, rocking his hips without moving his length so that she felt as if he'd completely opened her to him.

Spread wide like that she should've felt vulnerable, especially under his molten stare. Instead confidence and yearning sizzled through her system, urging her to again cup her breasts and pinch her eager nipples. He groaned and powered into her harder, the link of their gazes so strong she felt steeped in him. In and out.

Nothing else mattered but them, plastered together in the sultry night. With the jazz music swelling around them, and the breeze caressing their sweat-covered bodies with rain-scented, humid air.

She scooted closer and angled so that she could drop her head on the back of the couch, moaning when he drew her legs straight up and pulled them tightly together. Her toes flexed in the air as her needy sex clutched at him, her hips rolling up into driving strokes. He held her ankles in his hands, using them as fulcrums to bear down with more force, to slide through her slick walls and kindle the embers of her earlier orgasm.

Since she couldn't get her hands on him anymore, she dragged her nails over the leather cushions, not caring if she damaged them. Not caring if her moans seeped into the alley below her window. At that moment, anyone could hear. Hell, she wanted them to.

"You're going to come."

His voice invaded her mind, reaching her where she'd become a mindless mass of pleasure. She whipped her head back and forth, bumping it on the hard frame of the couch. Thank God for its wide padded arms, though she doubted she would've felt it if he'd been fucking her on a bed of nails. Her entire consciousness had centered on his plunges, each one dragging her further away from that safe place where she'd been before she met him. Now she was crazed and hungry, desperate for him to fill her up with his thick shaft. Wild for him to lay her bare and take what he needed, as long as he gave her back as good as he got in return.

Again and again he hit that spot inside her, the one that made her legs jerk and tremble in his grip, and she whimpered when he sank in deep and his balls slapped her ass. After that she didn't hear anything but her own endless moans, erupting from her lips while she bowed up to meet his downward slides. He pulled her legs up high, embedding himself to the root inside her, and she screamed, her sheath spasming so hard with her climax that he shouted an oath and followed her.

He released her ankles and slumped over, propping one hand on the cushion beside her head. The other caressed her breast. "It's that damn tattoo," he said, making her laugh. "I'm not responsible for my actions."

Lazily, she trailed a hand up his spine. When had she last felt so damn amazing? Oh yeah, the other night, when they'd been together on the roof. "So can we be irresponsible again soon?" She shifted to alleviate the twinge in her back from the awkward position crumpled against the sofa. Still worth it. "Please?"

His laughter saturated her senses, as thick and sweet as the afterglow shimmering over her damp skin. "Count on it, princess," he murmured, and she smiled into the darkness.

Sometimes being a princess wasn't so bad.

Chapter Seven

Alexa woke wrapped around Dillon, with their lips locked and his hand tangled in her hair.

His kisses were as slow and easy as the morning, and stirred her arousal effortlessly. He had the softest mouth and boy, did he know how to use it. Each time his tongue coiled around hers, pulling gently, she felt the answering beat between her legs. Already restless, she arched against him, well aware that his morning wood had grown. Now it was closer to the trunk of a magnolia tree, if she were inclined to be fanciful.

And when Dillon's mouth was making slow, masterful love to hers, she sure was.

"Mmm." Dizzy with longing, she rubbed against him. "Love morning magnolias."

He laughed and moved back, peering at her with narrowed eyes. "Did you just call me magnolia?"

"Did I?" In her current state, anything was possible. She flashed him a coy smile in the hopes of distracting him. "Maybe. I'm feeling awfully affectionate."

"Are you now?" He drew a fingertip along her jaw and down her throat, stopping at her racing pulse. "You look freshly sexed," he added, licking his lips in a way that triggered a whole new throb in her body. "Hair loose and messy, eyes sleepy." His finger resumed its journey, pausing at one of her tight nipples. Circling there. In the night, she'd donned her sleep clothes, but it didn't matter, because she felt naked all over again. "You're not one of those eager-beaver morning types, are you?"

She tossed her hair back out of her eyes and linked her hands behind his head. "Afraid so. I'm really eager right now."

"Is that so?" His hand crept under her cami, brushing the soft skin of her belly before sliding upward to tease the bottom of her breast. Another inch and he'd be stroking the taut tip without any clothing in the way. *Oh yes please.* "Eager enough to miss breakfast in favor of sex?"

Miss breakfast? She'd miss breakfast, lunch, and dinner if she got to stay curled around Dillon. Then she glimpsed the time on her bangle watch.

"Holy shit!" She leaped off him without warning, throwing an accidental elbow into his gut as she struggled to right herself. "Is it really almost eight-thirty?"

He tucked his arms behind his head and smiled. "Guess so."

"I need to get to work. The store opens at nine and there's a ton of stuff to do before then."

Most of the guys she knew would've made some crack about the boss being allowed to be late, but he only nodded and pulled himself to his feet. "I'll walk you over."

"It's only downstairs."

"We'll stop by the bakery first." His tone brooked no argument.

She yanked down her cami and compressed her lips. She should tell him no. Maybe even start extricating herself from this burgeoning so not a one-night stand before things got messy.

Then he folded her fingers into his callused palm and tugged her up for another kiss and she forgot all about suggesting they go their separate ways.

He watched cartoons while she got ready, laughing aloud at the antics of Stewie and crew on reruns of *Family Guy*. He'd made himself a bowl of cereal from her lone box of cornflakes, and munched them sans milk as if she'd presented him with haute cuisine—well, if such a thing existed for breakfast.

But his interest in cartoons and cereal ended the instant she stepped into the living room.

Dillon eyed her as if she'd donned a leather bustier and garters. "Damn."

"Do you like?" She did a little twirl, knowing full well she'd gone overboard for work. But damn, she'd enjoyed slipping into the short navy skirt and clingy V-neck top. Especially when she'd paired them with nude hose and heeled boots that made her legs good, even by her own critical standards.

Really good, if the glazed and slightly dumbstruck expression Dillon wore was anything to go by.

"I love." He pounced before she had time to prepare, taking her mouth with a suddenness that stole her breath and her common sense right along with it. Right now, throwing her arms around his neck and pressing her body against his seemed like the best idea she'd ever had.

She was in serious trouble.

"Mm, even your toothpaste tastes sexy." Grinning, he flicked his tongue along the corner of her mouth, digging into the grooves of her smile. "You look ah-mazing, Alexa. One-step-from-a-heart-attack incredible."

She laughed and stepped around him to collect her purse. "Thanks for the explanation."

"Since we're new friends and all, I figured you might need

help learning my personal lexicon."

"New friends who barely know anything about each other," she teased.

"Must be time for the big getting-to-know-you talk." He crossed his arms over his barrel chest and grinned. "I'm twenty-nine, single, standard set of parents. I own my own home, a Harley, a dented old boat, and a Silverado."

"Any siblings?"

He frowned. "One. A brother." Before she could question him further, he pressed on. "No kids. My hobbies are fishing, painting, and riding my bike." He scratched his scruffy chin. "Oh, and I'm a Leo."

"My psychic told me I was going to marry a Leo."

"Huh. I don't think we need to get fitted for matching wedding bands quite yet." He cocked his head. "You have a psychic?"

"She's my best friend Nellie's cousin." She shrugged. "Her specialty's the tarot."

"Interesting." But his expression said it clearly wasn't.

"You paint?" She tried to imagine this big, strapping, tattooed man's man holding a dainty paintbrush. Though she'd already seen him with the watering can. In his hands, daisies were sexy. "Really?"

"Really." He hesitated as if he was about to divulge a painful secret. "Watercolors. Not often anymore. I don't have the time."

"That's cool."

He only lifted a brow as if to say "yeah, right."

"I'm serious. I'd like to see some of your work sometime." She had to laugh at his dubious expression. "C'mon. Let's go."

It felt odd to follow him downstairs, and odder still to clasp his hand when he held it out. She should be rushing into the store to get her morning routine started, not taking the time to stroll in the sunshine as if her day were entirely her own.

Your only responsibility is to make yourself happy.

Pfft to that one. She couldn't just forget the promises she'd made to herself—and to Roz—even if Roz hadn't been around to hear them. For once she wanted to do something on her own, just to prove to herself that she could. This time, she was sinking or swimming all on her own.

"Penny for your frown." Dillon swung their hands between them as they made their way to the end of the street.

"Was I frowning?"

"Yes. You get the cutest wrinkle right here." He rubbed his finger between his eyes. "What has you worried on such a beautiful day?"

She glanced up at the deep-blue, cloudless sky. The bright sunshine made her squint, but she loved the warmth on her back and shoulders. Flowers bloomed all around them. Dandelions and wildflowers competed with clumps of pink mountain laurel and looked almost as beautiful.

And everything was so green. The vibrancy of the colors around her took her breath away, as if she were seeing the place for the first time. Even her own building, the one she'd decried as below her station, somehow looked tall and regal when she glanced back to ascertain her world hadn't changed overnight.

So if the world hadn't changed, what had? Her?

He squeezed her hand and she inhaled deeply. Hard to be depressed or anxious when a gorgeous guy with hair as gold as the day spinning out in front of them sauntered at her side. He hadn't allowed her to be alone when she'd been at the bottom of her own personal well.

No, for once, she didn't feel worried. All she felt at that very moment was grateful.

"It is a beautiful day. You're right."

"I often am. Remember that the next time you're tempted to argue with me." He pulled her against his side at the corner to wait for the stoplight to change. "So what's on the agenda today in flowerland?"

"Flowerland?" She smiled while they hurried across the street. Or rather, she hurried. Dillon's long legs ate up ground at their own lazy pace, as if he expected the world to simply wait for him to catch up. Looking as beachcomber-sexy as he did effortlessly, it just might. "A friend of a friend's getting married next year and she wanted to discuss Divine handling the arrangements. But I don't think it's going to work out."

They walked past Value Hardware, which already seemed to be moving at full-steam. One of the workers watered a hanging arrangement next to the door. Alexa frowned while the kid splashed water on the drooping red flowers. With some good soil, she could help that ailing geranium. It certainly wouldn't do well out in today's hot sun when the kid likely wasn't even soaking the roots.

Actually, he seemed much more interested in looking over his shoulder at Alexa and Dillon. A wide smile crossed his freckled face, and he opened his mouth to speak, but Dillon lengthened his stride, suddenly speeding up.

She smiled again. How sweet. He knew how she felt about that place and he didn't want her to have to see it for any longer than necessary.

He really was a nice guy. She didn't meet nearly enough of those. How strange that she'd stumbled upon him when she'd been at her lowest point.

Strange and sort of wonderful.

"How come you don't think it's going to work out?" he asked, voice slightly strained, once they'd made it past the sprawling hardware store.

"I don't have the staff, for one thing. My new floral designer just took another job so I'm on my own. Except for Nellie, the godsend. She's working with me part-time."

"That's good. Sucks about your other designer though."

Alexa shrugged. "Patty got a better offer. I can't really blame her for going. If I were in her position, I would've left too."

"No, you wouldn't." His quiet certainty caused her to stare up at him. Perspiration dotted his temples, but somehow that only made him look more rugged. She could so see him on a ladder, painting a house with his shirt off and all those golden muscles flexing. Those talented hips swiveling with his natural grace while he mounted each step, then turned to shoot her one of those dazzling grins that swept the thoughts from her head like sand from a bucket.

She shook herself out of her reverie. Whatever the positives to having Dillon around, he certainly didn't help with her concentration. "How do you know I wouldn't have left?"

"Because you're determined. You'd see the possibilities at Divine, not the problems. As you do now, even though you're frightened you're not enough to face them." He turned her toward him with a gentleness that made her heart race. "You are."

She swallowed and gazed up into his compassionate expression, wanting so badly to burrow into the safety of his embrace like he was her shelter in the storm. Her gut told her she could trust Dillon James.

God, she wanted to.

When she didn't respond, he tugged lightly on her hand and they started walking again, slowing at the attractively decorated windows of the bakery. "So you think the friend's event will be way too big for you to handle on your own?"

"I'm not set up for something that size. Even with temporary help." She pressed a hand over her stomach as it growled. "Eileen's inviting over a hundred people. I just don't think I could do it, even with a ton of lead time. Even if Nellie continues to pick up flower design as well as she has so far, I can't ask her to bust her ass when she's exhausted and dealing with swollen ankles."

"Nellie's your sister-in-law?"

"And best friend. She's very pregnant." Alexa sighed and dragged her attention from a fancy wedding cake. It was just making her hungrier. At least she had a granola breakfast bar with her name on it waiting for her in her desk drawer. "She's due in four months."

"That's great. You must be excited, auntie-to-be." He gifted her with another of those smiles he dispensed like candy and pulled on her hand. "Let's go in."

"Oh no, I shouldn't," she said weakly as he led her into the bakery.

The scents of freshly baked bread and vanilla washed over her in a comforting wave, and her stomach rebelled with another loud groan. She clutched her belly and winced.

"On a diet?" Without looking back at her, he urged her up to the huge, well-lit case of decadent treats. "Trust me, you don't need to. You're perfect as is."

"It's not my diet I'm worried about." Her gaze dipped to the price beneath a fat cranberry-orange muffin. Three dollars for a stinking muffin? Her lunch cost that at the deli down the street.

"Don't worry about anything, okay? Can you do that for me?"

She didn't reply to his low question as the older woman behind the counter bustled up to them. It wasn't as if Dillon could be in an incredible financial position himself. Handymen didn't make that much, did they? She honestly had no clue. Though he probably could afford a few muffins, right?

But when he bought half a dozen of them along with two cups of coffee—more chocolate raspberry for her—and various assorted treats the woman packed into multiple boxes, she raised an eyebrow. "You planning on feeding a battalion?"

He flipped out his wallet and withdrew a gleaming silver credit card. "I thought it'd be nice to leave some on the counter at Divine. And—" He broke off, looking uncharacteristically awkward. Then he covered his unease with a smile for the woman behind the counter. "Throw in a bunch of napkins, would you?"

She beamed. "For you, Dillon, of course."

"She knows you?" Alexa whispered when the woman went to fill his order.

"I come in here now and then." He shrugged.

Maybe handymen made more than she realized. He did seem to have a wide range of skills in that area. Perhaps he diversified enough to bring in a decent income. She bit her lip, considering his profile. Or could he be trying to show off a little? Maybe he'd suggest an expensive restaurant next and then she'd know he was wooing her.

Which didn't sound half-bad, truthfully.

Laden down with several white bakery bags, they entered Divine a few minutes later. She didn't have to unlock the door, which gave her a moment's pause until she heard the music flowing out from the back room. More jazz. She blew out a breath. Imagine that.

Dillon cocked a brow. "Who's here?"

Nellie came into the store with her arms full of gladiolus. She smiled over them at Alexa, her eyes alighting on the bakery bag she carried. "Oh, you brought donuts! Thank

God. I'm starving." Then she noticed Dillon and did a double take. "Oh, you brought more than that, I see."

Alexa gestured at Dillon and fought her sudden bout of nerves. Introducing him to her best friend made all of this more real somehow. Too real.

"Nellie Conroy, this is Dillon James." She flailed for an appropriate introduction. God, what should she say? "He's, um, my apartment building's handyman. Dillon, Nellie."

Judging from the narrow-eyed glance he gave her, she shouldn't have said *that*. Terrific. Yet another flub to add to her growing list.

As annoyed as he clearly was at Alexa, he was all smiles for Nellie. "Hi. Nice to meet you. Here, let me give you a hand with those."

Before Nellie could say anything, he'd swept the flowers out of her arms and laid them down on the paper-covered prep table behind the checkout counter. "These smell good," he said, his agile fingers plucking through the long-stemmed flowers with a care that made Alexa swallow hard. He didn't look at her, and she felt the loss of his teasing glances as acutely as a slap.

Dammit, she hadn't meant to hurt him.

"My name's actually Noelle," Nellie said, propping her hands on her hips. She gave Alexa the evil eye. "Though Lex and Jake can't seem to remember that."

"Oh, you're such a Nellie. Get over it already." To distract herself, Alexa set the bakery bag on the counter and tucked her purse behind it. Then she drew out her morning checklist and noted with a mixture of pride and concern that Nellie had already checked off a handful of things. Those were her tasks. She liked going around checking on everything each morning, noting which flowers looked a little worse for wear, which she would have to baby. What she was low on, what she had too much of. How the different arrangements looked in the different slants of light from morning to afternoon. Straightening until everything was just so.

"Yeah, and you're such a type A." Nellie eased past her and snatched the bag. "That's Lex's nickname," she added before she bit into a blueberry muffin.

"Can't say it doesn't fit," Dillon said, though he clenched his jaw again the instant he caught her looking at him.

Had he really expected her to announce him as her lover? Just put it right out there like that? It wasn't as if they were dating. Not exactly.

Okay, so they kind of were. Did that mean she had to tell the world?

Apparently it did.

"So you were up early working at Alexa's," Nellie said into the silence. "Or up late," she added meaningfully.

The implication of her statement wasn't lost on Alexa, but she needed to get the day started. "Thank you for coming in early to open up," she said to Nellie, her tone brisk. "I got a late start this morning."

"And it didn't cheer you up any."

"She was plenty cheerful until she came in here."

"It's her game face." Nellie licked traces of blueberry off her fingers. "Can't smile at work. Not the big boss lady."

"Oh, stop it. We laughed all afternoon yesterday."

But that had been different. She hadn't felt Dillon's presence like ants marching up her spine. His subtle hurt over how she'd introduced him permeated her consciousness. She hated that her first inclination was to push people away. Push *him* away.

"Can't argue with that," Nellie said, propping her hands on her hips. Her ginormous engagement ring winked in the sunlight, reminding Alexa of everything her best friend had and she didn't. A man who loved her, who thought she'd hung the sun. A family. A contented life, where she wouldn't ever be alone to fight the demons in her head.

"I have stuff to do in the back," Nellie said, waving what was left of her muffin. "Thanks for the eats, Dillon."

"No problem." Once Nellie had disappeared, he looked down at the client list she clutched in her hand. "So you do have a mailing list, of sorts."

His voice still sounded colder than usual. She'd just have to work her way around to warming him up.

"This is a repeat customer list. I call them to try to drum up more business. They haven't asked to sign up for anything."

"So sign them up for your e-mail newsletter, maybe something you send out seasonally when you update your website. You still have that kid working on it, right?"

"Yes." She was too stunned he'd taken this tack with her again to say more. What kind of handyman had such a keen interest in business?

Maybe it's you he has a keen interest in.

"So have him put together a newsletter while he's at it. Simple enough for people to unsubscribe if they don't want it, and a lot less pressure for you." He tapped the paper. "Tell you what. I'll put this into a spreadsheet. Will make it easier all the way around." He took her shoulders and ushered her toward the back office. "While we're at it, we can brainstorm your goals for the shop. We can break them down by season, since you work that way anyway."

"Why am I doing that exactly?" she asked as he pulled out a chair in front of her laptop and nudged her into it. The back door thunked closed, indicating that Nellie must've retreated outside to allow them privacy. For their spreadsheets.

Good Lord.

"There's power in writing things down," he said, straddling

a folding chair backward. "I'm sure you carry stuff in your head, but getting it on paper will help you see how to break it down in steps. An action plan, if you will. Something you're already doing," he added, apparently noticing her slack jaw. "You're on the right path already. You just need to shore it up a bit. Have you given any thought to those ideas I mentioned the other day? The lower-end arrangements, the cheap impulse buys for the counter?"

"A little," she admitted, thinking of the window displays she still hadn't put together. She'd almost abandoned the idea as a waste of time when Dillon had steamrolled her with his flurry of suggestions, but since then, she'd found herself planning in every spare moment. "It's a lot to do. Without much staff."

"Action plan," he reminded her, tapping the computer out of hibernation. "Let's get everything down, then we'll start weeding out what will and won't work. After we add in a projected time line, you can discuss it with Nellie and get started."

She stared at him, caught between feeling hopeful at his contagious determination and affronted that he obviously believed she couldn't do this on her own. "This is my store."

"No arguments there." He tucked a loose curl behind her ear and roamed his gaze over her face. "I want to help you. Will you let me?"

Saying no would've been so easy. She had this. A lot of what he'd said she'd already considered, but she just hadn't moved forward with it yet.

Because she'd been wallowing. And he wouldn't let her, not any longer.

"I won't step on your toes. I promise." He slid his thumb down to stroke her lower lip. Her heartbeat stumbled from the heat in his eyes. "If you want me out, I'll butt the hell out, okay?"

She nodded before her stubborn brain had a chance to voice an objection. "Okay."

"Great." He grinned. "Let's get busy."

Her lips curved as he opened her spreadsheet program. His big arms seemed to dwarf her laptop, but he danced his fingers over the keys with the same skill he used on her body. "Promises, promises."

He slanted her another grin, his gaze still enticingly heated. "I always fulfill them."

They worked side-by-side for over an hour, setting up charts and graphs and a contact spreadsheet she couldn't wait to fill in. He had a way around the program, and could generate fancy pie graphs with a few clicks. Having that visual, along with his low encouragement in her ear, helped make envisioning her plans a lot more fun. Plus on the screen they began to take real, tangible shape. Thanks to him.

When his cell rang and he stepped into the front to take the call, she found herself eagerly inputting the information they'd discussed. Income projections, an actual line-by-line budget. She'd had no idea actually seeing everything in front of her would solidify her footing.

She was so wrapped up in her work that she didn't hear him return. "I'm sorry, but I gotta go."

"You do?" Disappointment came first, quick and overwhelming.

"Yeah." As she rose, he came up behind her and crowded in close with his big, toned body. "Make sure you eat something," he said against her ear. He placed the cranberry-orange muffin she'd been salivating over all morning on a napkin and pressed a quick kiss against the side of her neck. "I'll be back for lunch. Probably a late one."

"You will?" Her voice sounded shaky, very un-Alexa-like.

The parroting thing she was doing was annoying too. But she couldn't help it, not when his strong hips rotated against hers with the suggestion of things to come.

Preferably she'd be coming too. Under his hands. Just under him, period.

"Yes. I will." Another kiss, more lingering this time. Inflaming her skin until she knew her cheeks had to be flushed with the havoc he created inside her with merely a skim of lips. "Have a good morning."

He left with the other bakery bags under his arm, making her wonder who would be getting his treats while she waited for him to come back.

She closed her eyes and sucked in a lungful of air. *God, get a grip.*

"Well, then." Alexa opened her eyes to find her best friend studying her from the doorway. That she wore a shirt with grabby cat paws encircling her swollen belly didn't diminish the stern set of her lips. "You slept with him last night, didn't you?"

She couldn't stop her smug smile. "We didn't sleep much."

"I just bet. He touched you like a guy does after he's already been on the carnival rides and can't wait to ride again. When were you going to tell me?"

"Soon." Alexa sighed. "Remember how I told you he went to get a part? Well, he got it and when he returned, he—" She broke off at Nellie's snigger. "What?"

"Slid the key in the lock? Slipped the notch into the groove? Inserted the meat in the bun?"

"Ugh, stop it!" Alexa couldn't help laughing. "Besides, he may have…slipped that particular notch a couple times."

"Uh-huh. You like him. I can see it all over your face," Nellie said, sobering.

Alexa pulled off a corner of the muffin. Smelled delicious.

"If I didn't, do you think I would've slept with him?"

"No. You definitely wouldn't be letting him help with the store if you didn't. You also wouldn't be glowing."

"Am not," Alexa said, swallowing her bite of muffin. She immediately snagged another piece.

"Are so."

Feeling bolstered by the sustenance, Alexa let a sly grin creep onto her face. "Okay, maybe I am, just a little. We had a good night last night."

"Deets, deets!" Nellie leaned forward expectantly. "How many positions are we talking here?"

"It's about quality, babe, not quantity." Alexa flipped her hair over her shoulder. "Let's just say we christened my couch and how."

Nellie's eyes widened. "Really."

Alexa studied her friend while she nibbled on her muffin. "You look green. Spill."

"It's nothing. Honestly. Just that…"

"What?" Alexa demanded, fearing the worst.

"Jake and I sort of had our first sexual, uh, encounter on that couch."

Alexa shrank back. "Seriously? On my *couch*?" Thank God she hadn't known that before. It totally would've doused her arousal last night. Well, possibly.

"It's comfy." Nellie shrugged, her pursed lips sliding into a smile. "Great memories. Glad to see it's been good to you, too."

"Can we get back to work now?"

"In a minute. *Was* it good for you, too?"

"The muffin?" Alexa swallowed the cranberry that had lodged in her throat at Nellie's couch-sex admission. "Oh yeah, the very best."

Grinning, Nellie picked up a spritz bottle of water.

"Thought so."

· · ·

Dillon headed over to the donor house they were rehabbing on Spring Street and helped fill in on the roof for a missing crew member for a couple hours, then returned to the Rison to put the finishing touches on the flooring in the apartment down the hall from Alexa's.

After that he checked on some of the other things on his list. The AC system did have a leak, one he'd have to fix soon. In the meantime, more refrigerant kept the place bearable. The stopgap measure was a waste of money, but he didn't have time to spare at the moment.

When he couldn't stall any longer, he took the baked goods out of the cooler in the back of his truck and headed over to Value Hardware.

He took the back way, feeling like a thief as he slipped into the side service entrance. The last thing he needed was to get caught dropping off pastries to the enemy camp by Alexa or Nellie.

See why this can't work? Your family's the enemy. Actually, you're *the enemy.*

"Dillon, how nice to see you." His stepfather grabbed him into a giant bear hug on his way down the hallway to the offices. "What's the occasion?"

The back of his neck prickled. "Do I need a special occasion to come by and see my folks?"

Truth was, he almost did. Minus his impromptu visit yesterday—which hadn't been for the purpose of family bonding—his visits to the store were few and far between. Something he intended to change, starting now.

"You don't come by nearly enough to suit us, that's all

I know." Raymond clapped him on the back and jerked a thumb at the bags Dillon carried. "What's in those?"

"I stopped by the bakery."

His stepfather grinned, his weathered face suddenly seeming years younger. He spent a lot of time out in the sunshine maintaining their family's property, and his nut-brown skin showed it. "Almond longhorn?"

"You know it." Dillon smiled and pushed the bag at him. "There's a muffin in there for Mom and a Danish for Cory, though I'm sure he won't eat it."

"That boy won't take a lunch to save his life." Raymond shook his head. "He's going to end up in intensive care if he doesn't let up."

Dillon scratched his chest and remembered the evasive look on his brother's face the day before when he'd asked about Melinda. Maybe Cory would be finding something—or someone—new to obsess about soon.

Like you have?

"He needs a woman," Dillon muttered. He should know, shouldn't he?

He'd found one that he wanted to get to know a lot better, and not just physically. What he'd learned about Alexa so far barely scratched her alluring surface. But how long could he hang on to the teeter-totter he was balanced on? How long until he ran into the wrong person at the wrong time and they blew his cover?

He never should've lied. Even with the acrimony between her and Cory, he'd had a better chance of convincing her he wasn't like his shark of a brother at the beginning than he did now. Now she'd believe he'd been scheming all along, likely for nefarious purposes. She'd probably think he was a spy for Value Hardware, intent on filling her head with business ideas he hoped were primed to fail.

"Speaking of women, have you found a date yet for the benefit?"

Dillon barely suppressed a groan. Not that again. His stepfather didn't tack on the word *appropriate*, but he heard it nonetheless. Problem was the dates he'd once considered more than adequate simply wouldn't get the job done any longer. Those sorts of women couldn't compare when he'd had the real thing and only craved more.

"No, I don't have a date," he said under his breath, knowing that would pry the lid off a can of worms he didn't want to touch.

"Why didn't you say so? You know Stanley Wren, my golfing buddy? His daughter's just home from Yale. She'd be perfect."

Terrific. Filthy rich, educated in an elite school, and young too. There was a winning trifecta in Dillon's book if he'd ever heard one. "I'm sure I can find someone."

"Well, if you can't find someone suitable," his stepfather winked, "just let me know and I'll get it set up with Haviland."

"Haviland?" Dillon choked. "That's a dish, not a person."

Raymond chuckled. "She's lovely. You'd like her. Why don't I give Stanley a call? You simply don't have time to find— "

"No." The sharpness of his answer made his stepfather do a double take. Damn, he needed to ease off. "I think I have someone in mind already," he said, softer now.

Did he ever. Now he just had to figure out how to keep her in his life long enough for her to agree to go with him.

"Your choice, son. Let me know if you change your mind."

They talked for a few more minutes while they walked through the store. His stepfather insisted on showing him a new pair of loppers he said cut through tree limbs like hot butter, and Dillon found himself chatting with a couple about the environmental benefits of a push mower over a traditional electric one.

By the time he swung by Cory's office to take him the Danish, his mood had vastly improved even considering he was still pissed at his brother for making Alexa cry the night before. He knocked and opened the door to see what looked like Cory's expensive Ming vase sailing through the air, hot on the heels of an ear-splitting screech, courtesy of Vicky. "God! You're a complete ass."

Cory hurtled to his feet in time to catch the vase, though he fumbled it a bit before clutching the artifact to his chest. "Have you lost your mind?"

"Yes, I have." She snatched up her books, sailing past Dillon with barely a muttered hello. "Only an insane person would consider working with you."

"You contacted me," Cory called after her, shaking his head and setting down the vase as if he couldn't quite believe what had just happened. "You again," he said, spotting Dillon.

"Women trouble?" Dillon asked mildly, fighting a grin.

Cory made a derisive sound in his throat. "Hardly. She's still a girl. What is she, twenty-four? No wonder she's such a hormonal wreck."

"You do realize that bringing up hormones in connection with a woman is reason enough to have your balls strung up as jewelry, right?"

"Gonna go tattle?" Cory tossed back, placing his vase on the sideboard with all the care of an indulgent father cradling a newborn.

"No. You're on your own with Vick." Dillon set the bakery bag on Cory's desk. "Danish," he said by way of explanation. "Eat something for a change."

"Aww. Bringing me sweets. I know you're not trying to get into my pants, so what's the occasion?"

Dillon leaned forward and placed his hands on the blotter, leveling his gaze on Cory's. Time to start laying it on the line. "Give Alexa some time."

Chapter Eight

One of Cory's dark brows winged up. "For what?"

"For her to get her affairs in order at the store. I know you wanted to slide in Melinda," he grinned when Cory's jaw went tight, "but if you give me a chance to make this work with Alexa, I'll get the place down the street ready for the yogurt shop. It'll be even better than Alexa's store when I'm done."

"Oh, really. Since when are you the wheeler and dealer in this family?"

"Since it's damn well time I step up and do my part."

"So you're helping Alexa just for the good of the company. And possibly your dick."

"Believe what you want," Dillon said easily, recognizing bitterness when he heard it. He also saw it written in the lines around Cory's eyes and the shadows under his eyes. Damn, he was about to extinguish his candle completely, from the looks of it. "Are you sleeping at all these days?"

"Somebody's got to handle things around here now that Mom and Dad are pulling back." Cory dropped in his chair and rolled up to his computer.

"Yeah, well, I'm here. I'll be here a lot more from now on," he added when Cory shot him a dubious glance. "Just give me some room with Lex."

"Don't you mean 'a room'?"

The juvenile joke would've made him roll his eyes, if he hadn't known it was Cory's attempt at putting another crack in the frost that had existed between them for years. As was digging out the cherry Danish Dillon had put on his desk, though he gave it a sniff when cherry smeared his fingers.

Dillon chuckled. His older brother definitely had his fussbudget ways, but damn if he didn't love the lug.

"You've got time," Cory said, not looking up from his pastry.

"Thanks. I appreciate it."

"No thanks needed. It's your company too, and I don't even like fro-yo." At Dillon's grin, he waved his hand toward the door. "Don't you have leaks to plug up? You're screwing with the feng shui in here." Then he winced. "Good Christ, she's rubbing off on me. Next I'll be talking about the aura of my leather settee."

Laughing, Dillon walked out of his office and down the hall, his mind already on lunch. Eating, however, wasn't what had him so excited, despite the gnawing ache in his gut. He'd scarfed down a couple muffins before laying the rest of the laminate flooring, but he'd still been hungry afterward. And not just for food.

After a quick stop at the deli to grab a couple sandwiches, and another coffee for Alexa—Irish cream this time—he headed up the street to Divine. The music hit him first when he opened the door. They'd switched to something with mournful strings and sweeping violins. In contrast with the scene of hilarity taking place near the prep table, the effect was jarring.

"Trying out bondage, ladies?" he asked as he set his bags and the coffees down on the counter. Then he unhooked his tool belt—he never remembered to take the damn thing off—and set that down as well.

Alexa pulled a pin out of her mouth and poked it into the bright pink ribbon sash she'd tied around Nellie's bulging midsection. "Ha ha. No, I told Nellie I'd make her a sash if we got through a bunch of the boutonnieres we need to get done. It's a rush job another florist botched so they have to be perfect. She totally rocked it."

"Way to go, Noelle."

Nellie beamed at him, probably for using her given name. "Thanks. Still can't believe a school's actually springing for a dance *before* school starts up again, but apparently their back-to-school mixer is a big hit every year."

"It's for Haven Prep, the middle school," Alexa added. "You know, the richie rich kids."

Yeah, he knew. He'd attended that school. "Aren't boutonnieres something guys get on their own?"

"They hired a florist to do corsages and boutonnieres for the kids to pick up as they entered the dance. Apparently they didn't want to take chances on what people would buy. They got the corsages from the other florist, the one who didn't get their colors right." Alexa shrugged. "Whatever floats their boat and pays green works for me."

Dillon studied the neat piles of flowers stacked across the prep table. "Wow, you've been busy."

"She's a whiz kid. Second day on the job and already kicking ass."

"Watch it." Nellie cupped her belly. "No swearing around the kid."

Alexa leaned down and spoke close to Nelly's stomach. "Your mama's kicking booty, girl child Conroy. Hear that?"

Nellie's giggle had to be one of the sweetest sounds he'd ever heard. When combined with the quick smile Alexa shot him as she straightened, he nearly staggered back. He loved seeing her happy. Way too much.

"I brought you guys lunch," he said, resting a hand on one of the bags. "Grabbed turkey sandwiches at the deli. Hope that's okay."

"Thank God." Nellie made a beeline for the bags, though she bypassed them to lean over the coffees. She took a long, dramatic sniff and sighed. "Ah, caffeine. I miss you so."

"What you've given up to reproduce." Alexa nudged her friend aside and snatched the coffee with the big A on the cup. "You're spoiling me, James," she said before taking her first experimental sip. Then her eyes rolled back in her head. "Holy Christ, this is delicious."

"Language!" Nellie danced away, hip-swaying into a rockin' boogie that didn't really match their musical selection.

Dillon frowned. "Should she be doing that? She might shake the baby loose or something."

Alexa laughed at his low comment. "Nah, that kid's gotta bake for months yet. No early arrivals will be happening on my watch."

"Absolutely not." He shuddered at the thought.

"Are we going to take an actual lunch break for once?"

Alexa rolled her eyes at Nellie. "You've worked here two days. Stop acting like you're dealing with horrible work conditions."

"Hey, let me do that," Dillon said, rushing forward to help Nellie pull a foldaway table from the wall.

"I'm pregnant, not incapacitated," she grumbled, stepping aside just the same.

He set up the table in the small open space in the prep area and they spread out with their lunch. Alexa stiffened each time a customer came into the shop—which happened twice—but she slipped into her business mode without faltering.

While Alexa led a customer over to the glass-fronted refrigerated case, Nellie leaned close to Dillon. "She's a tough nut to crack, but don't give up on her. I guarantee she's worth it."

He didn't doubt that for a second, but the benefit was coming up fast. Once the gala talk overtook over the town, the chances of his remaining handyman Dillon James in her eyes were nil. This whole pseudo-relationship was living on borrowed time—probably why it felt so incredibly precious.

That's not why, and you know it.

"You've been friends a long time," he said instead.

"Yeah. Since high school." Nellie toyed with the pop-top on her caffeine-free soda. "She's had a rough year. First me and Jake, then Roz. She needs someone in her life, Dillon."

"She has you," he said, fully aware of what she meant. But he couldn't face the hope in her trusting eyes when he was nothing but a deceitful jerk. Worse, a deceitful jerk sinking deeper by the moment.

"She does. And I'd do anything for her, but I'm not there for her in the middle of the night. She's terrified everything's going to shatter around her." She glanced at Alexa as she chatted animatedly about the small pots of tiny silk red and white flowers she'd set by the cash register.

"They're great for offices, when you need a little cheer to spruce up the space," Alexa said to her customer. "I'm thinking of doing actual arrangements in the same style, so that people can have a real one for home and the faux one for work. Helps make the day brighter, you know?"

"Oh yes, I do. That's a great idea!"

Dillon smothered a smile as he glanced back at Nellie,

who cupped her stomach while she watched Alexa. "You okay?"

"Yeah." Nellie smiled. "Mother Hen syndrome. It waxes and wanes. Would help if you agreed to marry her and love her always." When he started to cough, she giggled and leaned forward to thump him on the back. "Sorry. Kidding." She beseeched him with big eyes. "Though you could get your wedding flowers cheap. Just saying."

He had to chuckle. "I'll take that under advisement."

His phone rang and he pulled it out, seeing the number of his event planner, Julie. She usually didn't contact him unless she'd hit a snag with the benefit, which he absolutely did not need. "I have to take this. Sorry." When Nellie waved him off, he answered the call.

They chatted about the usual sort of thing—ways to motivate more donors to contribute to the charity auction, advertising possibilities, and an issue with the caterer—and he wondered why she hadn't just waited until their next planning meeting. Now that the benefit was getting closer, they'd scheduled more of them to finalize last-minute details. He'd blown off the last couple of them, because he'd been busy. With Alexa.

As much as he loved the benefit, he didn't regret spending the time with her. It was way too precious.

"I know you don't have a date for the gala yet," Julie said, drawing his attention. "Neither do I." She lowered her voice seductively. "We could be good together, Dillon."

His gaze shot to Alexa, still occupied with her customer. But she wouldn't be for long.

"I can't. I'm sorry. There's someone else." Someone he'd finally decided to ask to come with him to the benefit. He didn't want his stepfather to set him up with some china dish. He wanted—no, he *needed* Alexa to be at his side.

He just had to come clean first. And hope she didn't tell him to go to hell.

"I asked around and everyone says you're not seeing anyone," Julie said.

He hissed out a breath. What the hell was she doing, running polls about his sex life? "I don't check in with the town when I sleep with someone."

She chuckled. "You used to enjoy having everyone see what gorgeous woman was on your arm now. What's wrong with this one that you need to hide her away?"

"I'm not hiding anything," he snapped, louder than he'd intended. Remembering Nellie, he glanced up to see her glaring at him.

Fucking fabulous. Could he dig his hole any deeper?

Once he hung up with Julie, he leaned closer to Nellie. "I'm asking Alexa to the Helping Hands benefit. I just haven't had a chance yet." If he told her the truth first and she realized he'd only wanted to help her, maybe she'd even *want* to go with him.

Hell, a guy could dream.

She nodded and firmed her mouth. "Don't hurt her, Dillon. If you can't do right by her, just end it now. She cares about you, and she's way too fragile to deal with anyone's bullshit."

"I know." He shut his eyes. "I'm not going to hurt her," he said, and prayed it was true.

• • •

By the time Alexa made it back over to Dillon and Nellie, the happy mood at the table had cooled considerably. Before she could begin to figure out why, Nellie bounced to her feet and claimed she need to pee "something fierce."

Not about to get in her best friend's way on that matter, Alexa sat beside Dillon and picked up her abandoned sandwich. Her appetite had deserted her as usual, but she couldn't deny the sandwich tasted great.

The pensive look on Dillon's face, however, didn't go down half as well.

"What's the matter?" Alexa murmured, almost afraid to ask. Were Nellie and Dillon already not getting along? Everyone and their little doggie loved Nellie. "Problem between you and Nellie?"

"No." The smile he gave her soothed her concerns. Mostly. "Why would there be?"

"No reason. She just looked a little green when she ran out of here."

"She is pregnant." He sounded almost defensive.

"Yeah." Alexa picked at her sandwich, surprised by her disappointment at the possibility of friction between Dillon and her best friend.

It wasn't as if she and Dillon were anything serious or even really anything at all. The past week had been fun, sure, but they weren't long-term material. The guy enjoyed manual labor and got off on spreadsheets, for pity's sake. They were from different worlds, completely opposite poles. They'd stumbled over some emotional common ground here and there, but that had been accidental. And temporary.

Keep trying to convince yourself.

Suddenly aware that he was staring at her, she blurted, "Where do you fish?"

"There are a couple places, but most often Gillie Lake. East end, near the woods. There's this pier that's just big enough for me and a couple of other guys. It's a quiet spot."

"Thought you had a problem with eager-beaver morning types."

"Actually I fish in the afternoon, usually around twilight." He rubbed his nose against hers until she had no choice but to grin. He had that effect on her way too often. "When it's a clear night and not too hot, that's where I go."

She almost asked what entertained him about getting chewed up by bugs and then carving up an innocent creature when he could get one already cleaned and ready to go at the grocery store, but she bit her tongue. It was far too early in their not-quite-a-relationship to show him her crazy. "That's nice," she said instead, pretending not to notice how his lips twitched.

"What time do you close today?" he asked, his voice husky.

"Eight." Her own came out scratchier than she expected, so she cleared her throat. God, what those jewel-blue irises and inky lashes could do to a girl if she wasn't constantly on guard. "I stay open later on Fridays because we close at two on Saturdays. Roz was convinced that a lot of people appreciated the shop being open later on Fridays because of last-minute dates."

"Eight, huh?" He leaned close and his scent wafted over her, aftershave and the faintest hint of laminate. Damn if it didn't make her nipples harden. "If I come back then, will you spend your night with me?"

She swallowed the rush of excitement his words caused. "The whole night?"

He smiled. "As much as you can handle, Conroy."

Right then she could've tackled him and ripped off all his clothing without batting a lash. "Sounds like a plan." Then she smiled, suddenly eager to throw him as off-balance as he'd been so easily making her all week. "Though you could sweeten the pot a little, if you wanted."

His eyes fired with interest. "Oh yeah?"

"Yeah." She grinned as Nellie reemerged from the bathroom, sash miraculously still in place. "You could help us."

. . .

By the end of the afternoon, she had to hand it to Dillon. He didn't give in easily.

He stuck with her and Nellie, fumbling through making boutonnieres. They consisted of a red carnation, a spray of greenery, and baby's breath, wrapped tight with green floral tape and finished off with a small yellow bow. She and Nellie could fly through them, mainly because their fingers were nimble and quick. But Dillon, who worked with his hands day in and day out, seemed all thumbs.

That he had to take half a dozen phone calls didn't help with his learning curve. The guy was in serious demand. He must be doing much better as a handyman than she'd assumed. Considering his amazing business sense it wasn't too much of a stretch.

More than once she asked him if he needed to leave, but he waved her off. And then answered another call.

Finally they settled into a routine. Dillon worked without complaint, even occasionally singing along in a falsetto to the songs in Nellie's pop mix CD.

A couple times, customers wandered in and usually wandered out just as quickly. One of them left behind a ripped-out page from a women's magazine that she'd probably return for later. It depicted a fall arrangement that looked like a home art project: a vertical foam cone wrapped in glittery leaves and streamers, with yellow and orange blooms behind it. Not the kind of thing Divine carried, that was for sure. They kept everything high-end. Too high-end, some claimed, like the magazine clutcher from that afternoon.

And that was even *after* she'd put out the little teaser items on the front counter as Dillon had suggested.

"Cute, isn't it?" Dillon picked up the page Alexa had tossed aside. "Looks fun to make."

"You had trouble with a simple boutonniere."

"I got the hang of it eventually. You underestimate the skill involved in what you do."

"You twist a couple stems together and wind in a ribbon. No skill involved." All right, so that wasn't true. She needed to get over her low self-confidence thing. She'd never had that problem before the past year.

"So wrong." Idly, he tucked a loose strand of hair behind her ear, his gaze still on the craft project. "These could really drive in traffic. They'd be cheaper, and the customer could customize them depending on the flower they chose. You could do all kinds of things with them. I know, my—" He broke off, his Adam's apple jerking. "I bet my mom would love one."

Disturbed he'd arrived at the place she hadn't felt comfortable going herself, she snatched back the magazine. "This looks like something a grocery store would sell."

"Maybe. But that's because it's accessible." He rested his hand on the small of her back. "In this economy, that's what people want. They want pretty things just like anyone else, but they can't afford to spend a lot of money on them. So you appeal to every kind of customer, then when their money situation improves, they'll be back."

Logical. She couldn't deny that. But right now, she wanted to be stubborn.

Still, what would it hurt to do a couple of them and put them on the counter? Thanks to her trip to the craft store the other day, she had the stuff for the fall window displays she hadn't made yet. This would actually work perfectly with what she had on hand, and she could add her own flair to this basic design. All she'd need to get were the foam cones, or something similar.

Why not give it a shot?

She glanced at her watch. A few hours 'til closing meant they'd have to do something to keep busy, since they'd already finished with everything on her agenda for the afternoon. Including the boutonnieres.

"Thank you for your help," she said, turning at the sound of the cold case closing. Nellie had finally put away all the flowers, so they'd be moist and fresh for Haven Prep's formal tomorrow night. The party coordinator would be coming by bright and early Saturday to pick them up, though Alexa could tell she'd doubted a shop the size of Divine could get the job done. But Alexa had been prepared to pull out all the stops, even calling in her parents and Jake if necessary.

Luckily she and Nellie—and Dillon—had gotten the job done just fine.

"You're welcome. Even though I suck." His sulky expression made her grin.

She cupped his cheeks and pulled him down for a quick kiss. "You blew off your whole afternoon to stay here with us and I know you had a ton of stuff to do. I really appreciate it."

"No biggie."

"Will you get in trouble for not being available?"

Something slipped through his gaze before he shifted to kiss her fingertips. Just that simple gesture set her toes tingling. "Nah, it'll be fine. I'm actually due back at a donor house this afternoon. Remember that roof I mentioned yesterday? I do volunteer work as part of the Helping Hands charity." She didn't quite get why his voice lowered, and his brows pulled tight. "A lot of work for them actually. They provide houses for disabled vets or disadvantaged families, as a way to help get them back on their feet."

Warmth blossomed in her chest. He must have an understanding boss, if he let Dillon fit in volunteer work around his regular duties. Unless Dillon was self-employed. He'd never said. "That's great. If you need to go, it's okay. I have Nellie."

She glanced up as Nellie rushed toward them, cell clutched in one hand. "Sorry, I've gotta go. Jake's coming by any minute and he scored tickets to tonight's show at the civic center. It's a knockoff of Cirque du Soleil. I've been dying to go, but it's been sold out forever."

"No problem." Alexa smiled and mentally shifted her plans. So much for picking up the foam things. She couldn't leave the store unattended. "Have a good time. And thanks again for all your help. You're a lifesaver."

"It was fun. I'll see you tomorrow?"

"I can handle the store on my own tomorrow. Enjoy the show, and I'll see you Monday."

"Awesome. Thanks. Have a good weekend." Nellie looked between them, her brows drawing together. "Both of you."

Dillon's phone beeped. "Sorry," he said, glancing at the readout. "Duty calls."

Alexa nodded and affixed a bright smile onto her face. Boy, he was definitely a wanted man, and not just by her. "Sure thing. I'm good."

He frowned at the moody gray sky beyond the front windows. "Where'd the sun go?"

"We're due for storms tonight."

"It's been one after another lately. You have a generator here?"

She didn't know whether to growl or smile at the concern in his tone. "Yes." With a light shove, she nudged him toward the door. "Go do your manly thing."

His mouth crooked into a half-smile as he looked back at her. Lingeringly. "I'll be back at eight. Wait for me."

"I will." She returned his smile—and his kiss when he bent to brush his mouth over hers. She shut the door behind him, her smile spreading. A night with Dillon promised to be very interesting indeed.

. . .

One night turned into two. Then three. Somehow before she knew it, they'd spent a whole series of nights together. He usually didn't get to her place until late since he seemed to work all the damn time. That he arrived fresh from a shower and usually with the glow of the sun on his cheeks was a happy bonus.

It wasn't just about the sex either. They talked. And laughed. God, did they laugh. Night before last she'd helped him put together a scale model of his Harley-Davidson, and he'd helped her decorate her apartment a little more. Which had mostly consisted of nailing pictures and kissing and more nailing…

Last night he hadn't been able to get away from the donor house he was working on, so she'd kept busy making arrangements to fill the hours he wasn't around. Not that she'd noticed his absence or anything. She'd—wisely, it turned out—followed through on his suggestion for the fall design. She'd already had to make more cones twice over, so she raised the price by fifteen percent. It was still more than reasonable, proven by how fast they sold out.

By Wednesday afternoon, she'd made half a dozen more with Nellie's help, plus a couple specialty ones with fancier flowers, more greenery and a slightly inflated price tag. Travis did a splashy poster for the front window—she shuddered only a little—and they sat back to wait for more customers.

They came, with money in their outstretched fists.

It was freaking unreal. She needed to implement some of Dillon's other suggestions in a hurry, since the guy clearly knew what he was doing. Must be a natural at business or something.

Alexa faced her web designer with her hands on her hips. "I need that site done," she said in her sternest voice, unwilling to be fazed by Travis's slightly adoring gaze. "I want it launched within two weeks. There's online business we're missing." *And that way if this place gets foreclosed, I'll still have a storefront.* But she didn't say that.

"I'm on it."

"And that newsletter we talked about?"

His puppy dog look made her sigh inwardly. "On that too."

"What about those sales projections for next spring? Were you able to input them?"

"Once I figured out your chicken scratch, yeah. The graph you set up is pretty sweet. Makes it almost effortless."

More points for the handyman. "Thanks, Trav. I appreciate it."

Once Travis disappeared into the back, she sighed happily. Things were going well. So well, in fact, that when the phone rang and she snatched it up, she almost chirped her standard greeting.

"Hey, princess."

A grin stole across her face at Dillon's voice. "Hey, stranger."

"How are you? You sound happy. Business going okay?"

"Better than okay. Fabulous actually."

"Really? Tell me."

"I'd rather tell you in person." She heard a muffled yell behind him and slitted her eyes. "If you can get away."

He swore under his breath and she heard a muted conversation take place between him and someone else, presumably the yeller. "I'd love to, but we need to put the finishing touches on this place today. There's this benefit coming up…they want to unveil photos of the finished house."

"The Helping Hands benefit," she said, smiling at Travis as he waved and headed out. "It's all over town." The yearly gala was a pretty big deal. Amazing that the house Dillon had been busting his ass on was going to be featured. Equally amazing that he gave back so much to the community.

She resisted a little sigh. He made her stomach quiver. Either that or the soup she'd had at lunch was off. But no, it was Dillon. Had to be.

His pause hung heavily on the line until he hissed out another oath. "Yes. Hang on a sec, baby. All hell's breaking loose here."

"Sure." *Baby.* He'd called her baby. And she wasn't screaming at the term. Clearly she'd made major progress.

Or else she'd reached the point of no return. Next they'd be spooning and calling to say "I lo—like you" just because.

"Okay, sorry. It's always nuts at the end."

"I can see you tomorrow—"

"No. I already missed a night."

She couldn't suppress her grin. So he'd missed her too.

"Can you come by the house later? When the store closes?"

"Your house?" This was big. They hadn't quite made it there yet. Maybe the place was tiny or rundown or something, though with his skills she didn't see how that could be possible. He could probably turn a shed into a chalet.

"No, the donor house. I'd like to show you around. If

you're into it," he added, suddenly nonchalant.

Her smile grew. "I'm into it," she said softly and wrote down the address he gave her.

After closing, she went upstairs to her apartment and packed a soft-sided cooler with her brass candlesticks, a checkered tablecloth, and an alfresco meal for two. She had no idea if the house had room for them to have a picnic, but she'd love to share a meal with him outdoors even if it took place on the tailgate of his pickup.

She grinned at her reflection in her rearview mirror as she put her car in gear. Imagine that. Alexa Elizabeth Conroy, picnicking and pickupping with a guy she was sort of in a relationship with. Who'd've thunk it?

Falling for Dillon—and she couldn't deny she was, because even accomplished self-deluders had to have a break-even point—had been the easiest thing she'd ever done. Somehow he'd been there to shore her up when she'd started to crack, and for that she owed him. Hell, it was partially due to him that she'd gotten such an insanely amazing job that afternoon and would be working her ass off to meet her deadline.

Her mouth curved. She intended to show him her gratitude handsomely tonight.

She found her way to the house and parked at the end of the drive behind a sprawling motorcycle. There were no other vehicles around. No noises of construction workers, which she had to admit she was a little disappointed about. Considering she'd never been to a work site before, it seemed just cruel for her not to get to see at least one buff, sweaty man.

Hauling the strap of her cooler over her shoulder, she shut the door and glanced down at herself. Her pencil skirt and off-the-shoulder top probably weren't the best for picnicking. At least she'd thought of bug spray, which she'd applied liberally after slathering her bare shoulders, neck, and face with sunscreen. It had to be ninety degrees in the shade.

Then Dillon stepped out of the backyard, a long length of wood over one shoulder, and she learned what a hot flash really was.

"Hey." He grinned and stopped short, eyeing the cooler she held before turning his attention to her. "Damn, woman, are you trying to make me drool?"

"Fancy talker." She walked over to him and lifted her hand to his cheek. His eyes were so blue, like twin lasers that could see right through her. "You're all sweaty."

Apparently he took that as a suggestion to back off, but she snagged a handful of his wifebeater and tugged him right back. "Don't mind that?" he asked, setting down the lumber.

"I'd like to rub against you like a kitten in the sunshine. Unless you consider that weird. In that case, then yes." She gave a fake shudder. "Please don't sweat on me."

Laughing, he took her cooler and grabbed her hand as they strolled into the backyard. "I want to show you the house. Then we'll figure out that rubbing thing."

Her first impression was of abundant space. The yard was huge and fenced in white, the perfect inspiration for a romantic's dream. Lush green grass and a few perennials added to the feeling that the home was well tended, though the flowers looked less than cheerful in the heat. "You could do more with the landscaping," he said, noticing her focus.

"Cabbage roses would be lovely here. Spreading out from near the foundation. They're fussy, but they'd fit in perfectly with a cottage like this." She shielded her eyes from the sun and inwardly cursed at forgetting her sunglasses back at the shop. "A cottage with solar panels," she added with a smile.

"Yeah." He dragged his forearm over his forehead. "Just did those last week. We tried to honor the integrity of the original design, but so much of the house had to be replaced that I figured the benefits of adding them would offset the visual."

"They don't look out of place."

"Much," he teased, opening the back door and ushering her inside the cool, modernized home.

It was gorgeous. The home had exposed wood-beamed ceilings overhead, and pale walls and natural bamboo flooring throughout, which she identified without him telling her, much to his enjoyment. While they walked, he talked about quarried stone and low-flow fixtures and countertops made from a special resin that consisted of recycled content. His excitement spurred her own, and by the time they reached the front porch, she was grinning like a fool.

"You're like a little kid with environmentally sanctioned toys."

He glanced at her and smiled sheepishly. "I'm boring you."

"No way. This is so fascinating. I can't believe how much work you and the other volunteers have put into this house." And yet there was barely a sign they'd been there. Everything had been tidied up. The only evidence was the leftover southern pine Dillon had toted out to the side yard.

"We could've used you though, for the curb appeal aspect." He stared out toward the manicured front lawn. "You'd probably make these homes into showpieces."

"You've done that already. I'm so impressed, Dillon. Really."

"Thank you. I just hope John's happy here." He pulled her under his arm and brushed a kiss over her temple as they stared across the lawn. "His mom lives nearby. He's excited to spend time with her after his tours in Iraq."

"It's amazing. Truly."

"Amazing enough you'd go to the Helping Hands benefit

with me when they unveil the pictures?" His body braced as he asked the question. Did he really think she would say no? "It would really mean a lot to me if you came, Alexa."

She couldn't stop the grin that broke across her face. "I'd love to. I love what you've done to the house. And I love—" She broke off and bit her lip. "Sex," she finished.

That was better than what she'd almost said, something so utterly ridiculous and unexpected that she could only chalk it up to the heat and how impressed she was with his work. They barely knew each other. Weren't big feelings supposed to develop gradually over time, not burst up out of nowhere?

"Really. I never guessed." Lips twitching, he turned toward her and laid his hands on her shoulders. "Let's go grab that cooler from the kitchen and spread out in the backyard."

"Okay," she said weakly, though she wasn't sure more sun would help.

Sure enough, they were soon spread out in the backyard— but not with the picnic lunch they'd packed. The cooler still sat untouched on the edge of the tablecloth. No matter, Dillon had discovered a better feast than cold fried chicken.

Namely her breasts.

"I can't believe we're doing this," she gasped as he pulled her off-the-shoulder top and strapless bra down so that her breasts plumped over the top.

"I can. Jesus, I love this tattoo." He spanned his fingers over her breast and flicked his tongue against the dark pink nipple. "I'm dying to get inside you again."

It had only been a couple days, but it didn't seem to matter. She already quivered with need and he nudged her arousal higher with every lick. Every nuzzle and bite. "Me too. I want you so bad."

"You've got me."

He switched his attention to her other breast while

he dove his hand under her skirt to stroke her lace-topped garters. She wore them all the time now just in case, and he grunted his appreciation as he sucked on her breast. Then he was sliding a hand between her thighs, widening them despite the pencil skirt, and she whimpered at the brush of rough fingers over her satin panties.

Her very *wet* panties.

He shoved them aside and speared her with one insistent finger. Today he didn't take his time with foreplay. It was all about speed and urgency and impatient rubs over her throbbing core.

"So fucking slick. It's like you're dying for me too, that you can't get enough." He spoke against her cleavage as he played his fingers up and down her seam, torturing her with the light caresses before seeking out her tight bundle of nerves and thumbing the distended flesh.

The sunshine beat down on her scalp, on her shoulders, but she didn't care. She longed for him to experience the fever that consumed her. To feel it too.

She tugged at his shirt, wanting them to be skin-to-skin. His hard chest pressing against her bare breasts, his strong hips battering hers and stimulating that swollen spot he might as well have tattooed his name on, because it so belonged to him. She yanked his shirt over his head and tossed it aside, gasping as he gripped her waist and flipped her on top of him so that her breasts dangled close to his mouth.

"Ride me like this." He pulled up her skirt and tore her panties off her, then spread her thighs wide with his thumbs. "You're so wet, baby. Glistening in the sun. I wanna see it on me." He reared up and claimed her nipple, rolling it between his teeth while their gazes collided.

The crude talk didn't put her off. Instead it allowed her to give free rein to her own wicked desires. Especially since a damn near forest shielded their secluded "picnic" area from the neighbors. A definite plus.

She undid his jeans and shoved down his boxers, revealing the long, golden length of him. He seemed to harden even more under her perusal, and then the slow jerks of her hand as she worked him to a frenzy. Because she knew how much he got off on watching her, she made a show of circling the nipple surrounded by purple petals that drew so much of his fascination. All the while, she stroked his erection, pulling harder and harder until he arched his fine-as-hell body and grabbed handfuls of the grass above his head.

"You going for a quick finish, princess? 'Cause you're about to get your wish," he gritted, his arm muscles rippling to match the flex of his abdomen. And that beautiful cock, growing even thicker and stretching into her waiting grip.

"Uh-uh. No finishes unless they're in me." She licked her lips and his eyes almost rolled back in his head. "Or in my mouth."

"Goddammit, Lex. Suck me."

His growl streaked pleasure through her quaking, overheated body, and she couldn't comply fast enough. She lowered to her elbows and enfolded his shaft in her fist as she took a taste of him, one hungry lick from tip to balls. He lunged up off the tablecloth then sank back down, his arms extending again so he could pluck at the grass just beyond the tablecloth.

"Easy," she hummed against his erection. "Not your grass."

"Fuck, woman. Then stop teasing me."

She grinned. "But it's so fun." Even so, she took pity on him and slid her damp lips over the head, drawing lightly while she flattened her tongue and sipped his arousal. His massive thighs tensed and he pushed his jeans and boxers farther down, as if he wanted more of her skin against his. As if he wanted her still-partially-bound breasts to rub up against him while she sucked him and made him pant.

"Seeing you like this...in the sun...your mouth all the way around me and your nipples bouncing..." He couldn't seem to form sentences, but the picture he painted made her squirm and press her sticky thighs together. She pulled on him more strongly and reached beneath her skirt to where she was so painfully aroused that even her own fingers startled her enough moan out around his length. "Oh yeah, baby. Touch yourself. Let me see."

Some part of her couldn't believe she was rising to her feet and stepping out of her skirt so that she could continue giving her lover a blow job in the backyard of another person's house. In the sunshine. Where potentially anyone could see, if they had binoculars or excellent timing. Perversely, the idea of being caught only made her more excited.

She knelt at his side and took him in hand again. "Watch," she murmured, though he already was, leaning up on his elbows as she slid her fingers along her sex.

"Oh, I am," he grated. "Trust me."

Smiling, she darted her tongue over his cock while she teased herself. Gathering the moisture on her fingertips before slipping a digit inside. She knew from his low groan that he was studying the tight clasp of her body surrounding her knuckle. Swelling around it. She sucked him into her mouth again, farther than before, not balking as he knotted his hand in her hair and guided her up and down his rigid length. Never pushing her too far, just enough to thrill her even more.

"Enough." He let go of her hair and dropped his head back, the defined cords of his neck standing out at his rapid intakes of breath. "Fuck me."

"Since you asked so nice…" Alexa rimmed her swollen lips with her tongue and straddled him, making sure that his eyes were on hers as she sank down on his cock.

"Wait." She poised halfway down his length. "Condom?" he managed, and she shook her head.

"We're good." She moaned at his stiff flesh curving just right inside her, inflaming every nerve ending in her sex. "On the pill. You're clean?"

"Late now…to ask. But yeah. I am." He grabbed hold of her hips and levered off the ground, rocking all the way into her with a sure thrust that damn near blew her head off.

"Me too. Fuck, yes, that feels good."

She bowed her spine, her hair trailing over his thighs as he coasted his hands up her torso and palmed her breasts. And then they were skidding into madness, their hips slamming together, his pelvic bone hitting her clit just right to make her vision haze. She was on fire, the sun scalding her face and shoulders, heat scorching her from his deep, powerful strokes.

"God, you're beautiful." He rubbed her clit with his rough fingertips. "So sexy."

Goose bumps popped out on her skin, chased by the perspiration that made them both slick. His mouth seized her tattooed breast, the damp flicks on her tormented flesh more tinder for the blaze swallowing her whole.

When his mouth slanted over hers, she moaned, grateful for the supportive arms that wrapped around her while he impaled her over and over again. She dragged her nails down his back, drawing blood probably, shredding skin, but all she could do was ride him like he was the salvation she'd been waiting for all her life.

This wasn't just a quick outdoor screw. He made her feel so much, until she was sure she'd come undone from all the emotions rioting inside her.

Her heart didn't care how fast they'd crashed into bed. All it knew was that finally she had someone to hold her, someone to whisper, "let go, baby, I've got you," and she knew he did. He wouldn't let her fall.

Except on that score, it was already too late.

The fireball behind her eyes exploded, and she came in a blinding rush of pleasure. "Dillon." His name singed her lips an instant before he sealed his mouth to hers and fed her starved lungs with his breath.

She rocked on him with abandon, saturating him in her release, then yanking him with her when he couldn't hold on any longer. The last thing she heard was Dillon's shout as they hurtled into bliss.

Chapter Nine

Lying tangled together in the grass with the setting sun cooling their heated skin, Dillon thought he'd found heaven. She fit perfectly in his arms, and her head rested on his chest as if it belonged there. As if she would never leave.

"I'm freaking hungry."

He smiled and stroked her tousled hair away from her cheek. "I appreciate you bringing me dinner."

"Well, it was for me too, though I didn't really dress right for a picnic." She made a face. "I'm not exactly the outdoorsy type. I don't even own a pair of jeans."

His stomach sank to his knees. "So you probably wouldn't be up for fishing with me, huh?"

"Chances are high I'd squeal and complain the whole time, but I'd give it a try."

She was making it so easy to fall for her. Either that or he simply didn't have the power to fight gravity any longer. "For me," he said, swallowing hard.

"For you," she agreed. Her stomach burbled and she laughed. "Can we eat now?"

"Soon, I promise." Instead of sitting up to get the food, he tucked her head against his shoulder. He was so greedy for her. Just a couple minutes more. "I'd like to take you out on my motorcycle sometime. With your arms around my waist and no other sounds but the wind and the bike between our legs. You'd love it."

"Aren't bikes dangerous?"

"Only if you don't know what you're doing."

"And you do?"

"You know it, baby." She rolled her eyes at his smug grin and he couldn't resist cuddling her just that much closer. "Let me take you out on my bike."

She blinked, obviously still unsure. Her bluebonnet eyes wove a spell around him, and damn if he ever wanted to see his way clear. "When?"

His pulse bumped. Saturday was the night of the benefit. The days between now and then were growing shorter by the hour. "How's Friday?"

He'd go all out to plan a romantic evening and he'd finally tell her truth. Whatever it took, he'd make her sure she understood that all he'd wanted was to help her. Some of what he'd done might've been misguided, but his heart had always been in the right place.

As for the rest of him…that was up to interpretation. But she couldn't fault him for wanting her so much he couldn't think straight, could she?

Yeah. She probably could.

"Friday's okay. It has to be later in the evening, though."

"Right, the store's open late. That's fine. We'll take a ride, have dinner. Enjoy the evening."

"It might even be later than normal." A slow smile broke across her face. "Divine got a job. It's a quick turnaround too."

"Really?" Thrilled for her, he squeezed her against his side and dropped a kiss on top of her hair. "That's terrific. Tell me all about it."

"I will." She granted him a megawatt Alexa grin. And it was all for him. "Since it's all thanks to you. Well, mostly."

Curiosity piqued, he sat up and began to unpack the contents of the cooler. Then he lit the candles and sat back to view her lovely face in the flickering glow. "Going to tell me more?"

"It involves your brilliant idea, a party that suddenly wasn't complete without your brilliant idea on the tables, and a rush job that might lead to more if I can keep up with how fast your brilliant idea is selling. Guess I've turned into the queen of quickie jobs, but I don't mind that title." While he processed all that, she sidled closer and made a show of looking him up and down. "Eating naked? What will the neighbors think?"

"If they haven't already called the cops, I think they're probably open-minded enough not to mind."

She rewarded him with her soft laughter and an even softer kiss. Her taste careened through his system. Everything faded away but him and Alexa, and candlelight, and the sultry summer air that surrounded them.

Then she slipped back, eyes shimmering with the pink light of sunset, mouth wet and mischievous. Her smile widened at his expectant breath. "So what would you say if I asked you to help with that rush deadline I told you about?"

He grinned, already juggling his commitments in his head. He'd do whatever was necessary to make the time. "I'd say you owe me dinner if you want me to put out."

• • •

Over the next two days, he learned the meaning of true exhaustion.

He twisted, and shaped, and pinned until his fingers were numb. His "creations"—he couldn't in good conscience call them floral designs, though they did seem to improve as his volume increased—wouldn't win any awards. When he put them next to Nellie's and especially Alexa's, to him they stood out like sparkly thumbs. But Alexa just shoved more materials into his hands.

They kept going late into the evening on Thursday, then started again bright and early on Friday. Nellie brought her own form of ballast in the form of Alexa's older brother, Jake, who seemed to spend as much time watching Dillon as he did fumbling through his own arrangements. But the help was definitely appreciated.

It took all four of them working their asses off until after nine. Alexa counted up the arrangements, loudly declared the operation a rousing success, and immediately toasted Nellie with the sparkling grape juice she'd been holding in reserve. Then the two of them disappeared into the back room.

Jake cornered him before he'd even taken his first sip. Dillon would've been more prepared for his attack had he not been consumed with staring after Alexa. The black seams of her stockings climbing up the backs of her shapely legs had tormented him all damn day.

"I have a black belt in karate," Jake said in an undertone.

So much for pleasant reveries of licking his way up the backs of Alexa's calves. "Great," Dillon replied. "I, ah, have always liked Bruce Lee movies."

"I wanted you to understand who you're dealing with. I know you're banging my sister."

Dillon stared straight ahead, sure he'd misheard him. Maybe Jake had said seeing, which translated into banging in Dillon's mind. It was possible. "Excuse me?"

Jake let out an aggrieved breath. "Fine. Dating. Though it

doesn't sound like dating much to me. You fixed her sink, then what, you decided she could tip you with her body?"

How was he supposed to answer that one? "Of course not. We've been in church every night, despite what your wife's obviously told you."

He half-expected for Jake's fist to collide with the sparkling juice on its way to his face. Instead all he got was a low laugh. "Right. We spent some time in church ourselves before we got married."

The ladies returned with more sparkling juice, Nellie talking on her cell while exchanging hot looks with her husband. Alexa watched them with a wistful expression while she sorted through her endless reams of paperwork.

Now that Dillon had helped her create a few more graphs and charts, she had begun noting every supply she used on a checklist, right down to paper clips. She was an organizational freak's idea of a dream date.

When she glanced over at Dillon and winked, he had to shift at the sudden tightening in his jeans. Or a handyman-slash-business owner's, since he definitely dreamed about dating Alexa—and much more.

"Looks like it turned out pretty good for you guys," he said, tilting his cup toward Nellie.

"Yes, it did," Jake agreed, his gaze riveted on his wife. "But we had history. You and Lex barely know each other. And church or no church, biblically doesn't count."

Dillon smothered a laugh in a cough. "I hear you. You're right. We have a lot to learn about each other." He glanced back at Alexa and noticed she'd switched to sifting through her mail. Right on top lay the glossy real estate magazine that contained a spotlight on the gala this month—and featured him. *Shit.* "But I'm willing to put in the time. I want to," he added, already backing away from Jake.

Dammit, he had to get his hands on that magazine before he talked to her. Or else he wouldn't need to bother.

"So she's not just some random woman to you," Jake stated, his narrowed eyes never leaving Dillon. "You're not going to break her heart."

The first part was true. The second, he had little control over, at least anymore. What he'd set into motion could only be stopped with the truth.

So, basically, he was fucked.

He glanced at Alexa again and watched her run the eraser of her pencil over her mouth. So damn sexy. She could fondle a stapler and he'd get hard. Christ.

"She means something to me." Way too much.

Jake studied him for a moment longer, then nodded and tossed back the rest of his drink. "Look, I know what it's like to think you're not good enough for someone. It took Nellie a while to prove it to me." Jake's smile showed he was taking a trip down memory lane, and from his expression, he wasn't visiting the clean neighborhoods. "Lex'll convince you eventually. If you want to be convinced, that is."

Unsure how to respond, Dillon glanced down at his clothes as Jake ambled away. The guy saw him as the handyman in ragged jeans and a T-shirt, so naturally he assumed Dillon would doubt his attractiveness to an elegant woman like Alexa.

But what if he was right? What if part of the reason he hadn't yet come clean to Lex was because he wondered himself if Value Hardware—and by extension him—was the greedy, insensitive industrialist she'd accused it of being?

And if so, what the hell was he going to do about it?

"Attention everybody!" Nellie's voice rang out over the music and Alexa and Jake's voices. "My best friend has an announcement."

Dillon's stomach tensed. Now what?

Alexa beamed and waved a piece of mail that looked like a check. "Along with us kicking ass on the Yancy job—thank you very much—I got the money from the sale of the house today. So you know what that means, right?" She opened a drawer and withdrew a stack of papers. With a flourish, she dumped them in her wire trash basket and took out her lighter. "Time for these suckers to burn, baby, burn. Overdue? Screw you." She laughed and set the corner of one alight. "Only for a minute, I promise," she added at Nellie's anxious expression. "It'll be the smallest fire ever."

The environmentalist in him balked at the possible ramifications of starting a blaze, but that didn't explain the quick seizing of his chest.

She was burning the notices from Cory. From him, even if he'd never known they existed before a couple of weeks ago.

The sound of the flames licking the paper disappeared in a flurry of whoops and laughter, followed by the sound of a cork exploding. "The real stuff this time." Alexa grinned and poured the bubbly into her glass. "Sorry, Nellie. We'll celebrate for you."

He had to get out of there. Even his presence was tainting what should be a joyous occasion, because all he could do was stand in the corner and watch Alexa commemorate what might very well lead to the end of their relationship.

How had he believed he could just tell her the truth when it suited him? His reasons were just that—*his* reasons. Even if he'd been trying to help. Even if he'd wanted her to succeed so badly that he'd lost sight of what that might mean for them.

Even if he lo—

His phone rang and her gaze shot to him. Her vulnerability and confusion shone in her huge eyes. There were questions there, and the answers he'd been so ready to spill—so fucking sure he'd make it work, because it had to—were also on the verge of going up in smoke.

He glanced at his cell, then strode to her and wrapped her in a brief, tight hug. "Congratulations, baby," he whispered against her hair, unwilling to let her go. "I'm so happy for you."

"Me too. Thank you." She looked up at him and bit her lip. The gulf between them yawned wide, as tangible as the glass of champagne she clutched. "Want a drink?"

"I got a call. I have to go."

"Oh, okay. But you'll be back?"

The echo of what she'd said that day in her bathroom gave him another pang, this time square in his gut. "Yeah, I'll be back," he said quietly, already stepping away. He slid the incriminating magazine off the counter and held it up. "Mind if I borrow this?"

She frowned, but nodded. "Sure."

"Thanks. Have fun, Alexa. You earned this."

As he turned, he glimpsed the papers kindling in the garbage can. Smoke curled in the air, searing his throat.

Then Jake put out the minuscule fire and the flickers of flame went dark.

• • •

Where the hell was he?

There'd been some sort of weird vibe between her and Dillon when he'd left, but she knew he was thrilled for the progress she'd made. Not only was she starting to have an actual steady stream of business, she could finally pay off Cory just as soon as the money from her house cleared her bank. Everything was falling into place.

Including her relationship with Dillon. That's what it was—an honest-to-God relationship. They'd started to build something real and she couldn't wait to see what happened next.

If he ever came back, anyway.

To keep herself busy, she tidied the store and sprayed a little cinnamon air freshener to dispel the last of the smoke smell. It probably hadn't been the smartest move to set off a fire indoors but she'd needed to do something concrete to celebrate. She'd left the past in the past and she was moving on into her very bright future.

And she was a little drunk.

Not too much. Just enough to incite a buzz in her bloodstream. She couldn't wait to see Dillon. Tonight would be the best night of her life. She wasn't even scared to get on his bike anymore. Right now she wasn't scared of anything.

The jingle of bells made her glance up and grin. The sight of his welcome face and that spiky little crown of hair he kept mumbling about getting cut made her so happy that she charged him, taking him off guard as she leaped into his arms. He staggered, barely holding on to her, and she sealed her mouth to his, drawing on his full lower lip until he groaned. "Lexa, wait—"

"I like that. Lexa. So sexy." She bit his flesh and caressed the wound with her tongue. He tasted like the rain that had just started slipping down the windows and she could see the droplets beading on his temples. "Call me that when you're inside me. Here. Right here."

"Wait. No. Alexa," he said pointedly as he slid her down his body and her heels thudded on the parquet floor. "We need to talk."

But she wouldn't be dissuaded. She wanted her celebration, dammit, and she refused to see anything in his eyes except the arousal that had been on low boil inside her all day. There was nothing so important it couldn't wait.

"Do you understand what today meant to me?" she whispered, branding his mouth with hers. "How much I need tonight? Just. This." She punctuated each word with an openmouthed kiss against his stubbled throat and reached down to cup his stiffening cock. Ah, see, he wasn't nearly as reluctant as he pretended. Her abrupt touch ripped a groan from him and he reeled back, holding her at arm's length.

He stared into her eyes in the thin beam of light from the cold case, the only light she'd left on. The shadows swallowed his expression whole, but she could feel the way he tracked her face. First with his burning gaze, then with the backs of his fingers. Up the slope of her cheeks, over her temples. Along her quivering lips. The reverence in his strokes spoke to her, as if he were conveying without language exactly what she meant to him. How much she mattered.

How much *this* mattered.

"Goddammit, Alexa."

Without warning, he dragged her into his arms again. She shuddered as he sucked on the area between her neck and her shoulder, drawing with such powerful suction that her whole body vibrated. Moisture dampened her panties and her breasts swelled, nipples rising insistently against the soft cups of her bra.

She wanted his hands there. Not on her sides, sliding up and down. Her blouse whispered against her skin with his movements, another subtle torture.

When he whirled her toward the counter, she gasped and slapped her palms down to balance herself. She sensed rather than saw him kneel behind her. "What're you doing?" she managed when a flash of lightning blazed across the store and she reflexively closed her eyes.

He slid his hands up the front of her legs, his touch as silky as the ribbons they'd fought into bows that afternoon.

His thumbs eased into her heels, tipping her feet up. Then the pads of his fingers were sliding up the back of her legs, tracing the seam of her hose.

"All day," he murmured, nipping the hollow of her knee. She startled, nails digging into the counter. "All day I've watched you walk in these, and this seam taunted me. This line of black stretching from the soles of your feet up to heaven. You hiding it from my eyes under this." He toyed with the hem of her skirt, which might not have existed at all for how exposed she felt. "But I could still see you. I knew what you'd look like under here, and what you were saving for me."

She didn't speak as he rolled up the thin material. His sharp inhale upon glimpsing the lacy-topped hose and garters gave her a moment's enjoyment, then his teeth grazed her thigh and she forgot about everything but his mouth. His teeth. The pressure of his tongue. Her sex clutched around air and she cried out, the sound becoming a moan at the relief his lips offered.

He'd barely touched her and already she blazed for him. His fingers danced up and down the back of her calf, eliciting quivers she couldn't suppress. He tormented her with an easy expertise she really didn't care to dwell on, but she sure took advantage of it. Without hesitation, she rocked into his movements, as if he'd become her puppet master and she only existed to do as he bid.

An erotic thrill shivered up her spine at the sensation of his wide palms smoothing her skirt higher, baring the silk of her panties. He ran a fingertip around the scalloped edge and murmured words of praise she strained to hear. Just his voice made her quake.

Before this week, she wouldn't have called herself a romantic, despite making her living tending flowers. Creating the fantasy of a perfect, pretty, flower-filled world made her happy, but it hadn't changed the darkness she carried inside, that part of her that insisted happiness was something a person clung to before life and circumstance took it back again. But being with Dillon, more than anything else, made her believe. In romance. In hope. That not everything had to be difficult or hurt.

He'd shown up at the absolute worst time. Or the best, depending on her point of view. All she knew was that a week ago she'd been mired in worry and now, this very minute, all that bore down on her was sweet, sensual need.

Another clap of thunder shattered the web of intimacy he'd spun around them, until he nibbled the crease between her bikinis and the top of her leg and she jolted right back into that hot, dark space. He didn't speak, at least not loud enough for her to decipher what he said. Somehow that only built the intensity of the moment.

Slowly, so slowly, he crept toward the heart of her, where she craved his attention. Moans slipped through her parted lips. Her pulse pounded in her head. Between her legs.

When he finally brushed her mound, the cry that left her bordered on agony. That he followed that fleeting touch with another, then another still, didn't quell the ache. Only when he nudged aside the damp fabric and stroked her for real, worshipping her with every glide of his fingertips, did she expel the breath she'd held trapped in her throat.

"Oh, princess." His voice sounded as gravelly as rocks thrown against a window, and he panted just as she did. Amazing how that nickname now turned her on instead of pissed her off. She could hear his affection, savored it in his caresses. He traced the curve of her ass with his tongue, stopping just short of where his fingers continued to tease her. Dipping in and out. Sliding along her folds. Circling. Toying with her where she swelled for him. "I wish I could see you."

Half-tempted to draw her knee up on the desk to give him more room, she stared blindly at the sheets of rain slapping the windows. Fluttering the awning above the door, battering the roof. None of it had reached her consciousness before. How could it, when her heartbeat chugged in her ears and her body throbbed with utter awareness of the man who ruled her?

Lightning illuminated the shadowy room at the exact moment he plunged a finger inside her. She bit down hard on her lower lip to stifle a cry. "God, yes."

A noise outside made her jerk her head toward the door. With growing horror, she watched the knob turn and then a woman in a trench coat darted inside, a soaked newspaper draped over her head. "Oh, it's horrendous out there!"

All movement behind her—dear Lord, *in* her—ceased. And from somewhere she found the strength to whisper, "We're closed." *Can't you read the freaking sign?*

"Oh, I know. I'm sorry, but I thought I saw someone in here." She flapped her hand and her newspaper fluttered like a panicked bird. Much like Alexa's rampaging heart. "Though it's awfully dark in here. Can you turn on the light?"

"No." Then she repeated it again for good measure. "*No*. We're closed."

"But I forgot it's my grandmother's birthday and I need flowers."

Alexa blew out a breath. Figures she'd get a customer now. "There's some in that urn. Two fresh arrangements I did just this afternoon. Your choice."

Clearly perplexed, the woman selected a bundle in crackling purple tissue paper. It was a selection of stargazer lilies, lemon leaf and fragrant eucalyptus, set off with a gorgeous purple bow. The loss was worth it if the woman would just *go*.

"I have money," the woman began, hauling what Alexa presumed was a wallet out of her enormous bag.

"No, no, it's fine. They're on the house. I need to lock up." Forcing false cheer into her voice, Alexa added, "Thank you for stopping by Divine and happy birthday to Grandma!"

"Well, if you're sure…"

"I couldn't be more sure." She really could not. The stirrings between her thighs had pretty much made up her mind for her.

Dillon had pulled back, tucking down and shifting fully behind her. Thank God for the high counter. Though he remained close, he barely touched her now. Just his hands lightly cupping her ankles as if he knew she needed the support.

He was right.

"Say, are you going to the gala tomorrow night?"

Dillon's hands tensed and she swallowed over the tightness in her throat. "Yes. I'm excited about it." Manners dictated she reply politely. "Are you?"

"Definitely. I wouldn't miss it. The auction's usually great, and it's a terrific cause. Plus those hunky boys in tuxes make it worth my while."

Alexa fiddled with the picture of Roz she'd put on the counter that morning, just to give her antsy hands something to do. "Absolutely." *Go. Now. Please.* "Maybe I'll see you there then. Have a great night."

"You, too, and thanks. Good night." The woman clutched her flowers and flopped her newspaper over her head before fleeing into the storm.

"Fucking A, that was close." Alexa whirled to stare at Dillon, who wasn't grinning or laughing or even praying. "Dillon?" she asked as he rose and took a definite step away. "We weren't done."

His silence unnerved her, eroding the last of her desire that hadn't waned during the interruption. "I hope we're not," he said finally. He shook his head, his lips drawing into a flat, hard line. As if he was steeling himself.

"Alexa," he began, his expression grave. "We need to talk. It's important."

"Not tonight," she pleaded, reaching behind her for support. But there was only the cold glass of the counter. Solid, without warmth.

"Yes. I can't put it off any longer."

Ice scraped her throat. Whatever he was about to say, she didn't want to hear it. Not when she'd finally glimpsed the light at the end of a very long year, one filled with more pain than pleasure. He'd helped tip the scales in her favor and she'd be damned if they tipped back so soon.

She shut her eyes and clenched her hands at her sides, the only way she could stop from slapping them over her ears like a child who was afraid to hear the worst.

No. No. No.

"Baby, open your eyes."

When she did, he was right in front of her. So close she could meet his lips if she edged forward a little bit. His were moving, saying things that should've made sense had she still been able to hear over the buzz of white noise.

His eyes were so blue. She could just drown in them and float away, to a place where her happy flush of alcohol and success wouldn't fade at the first jolt of hard reality. She could fall in love there, just let herself go. She'd never hit the ground, not when he was with her.

"Alexa, did you hear what I said?" He stepped forward and gripped her shoulders, tugging her up on her toes so that their faces were nearly even. "I'm Cory's brother. I own—my parents own—Value Hardware. And—"

The buzz was back, encroaching around the edges of her hearing so that he sounded as if he were speaking through cotton. But she could see just fine. The sharpness of his expression, the hard planes of his face. The truth at the heart of all his lies.

"And this store," she whispered, the accusation tearing from her already aching throat. It was swelling with the tears she'd never shed in front of him. He didn't deserve them. He'd been given so much of her already, parts of her she'd never shared with another. Ones she'd never get back.

Now he was flinging them in her face.

"And this store." He closed his eyes and scraped his hand over the back of his head. The prickle of his hair against his palm cut through the hum in her ears and made her wince. "Goddammit, I hate the way you're looking at me. If you'll just let me explain, if you'll hear me out, I promise I can make this right. It's not what you're thinking. I care about you. So damn much. If you'd just—"

The laughter bubbled up inside her before she even suspected it was coming. It left her mouth on a sob that was closer to a dry heave than tears. "If I'd just what? Stand here and listen to more of your lies? You broke down every one of my walls, you bastard. They were so strong that no one ever got through. No. One." She lunged forward and beat her fists against his chest, barely registering the way he stood there and took the blows. Her face was wet, smeared with the hot fluid she refused to acknowledge was tears. They dripped off her chin, sneaked into the collar of her shirt. Imprinting her with her shame. "You were the only one I trusted. I shouldn't have. It didn't make any sense, how this could happen when I'd almost given up thinking it ever would."

"But it did. You feel it too."

"Too? Fucking *too*?" She raged, clawing at his shirt.

"You'd dare lie to me even now? How can you pretend to even know what a genuine emotion is when you're nothing but a goddamn fake?"

"What I feel for you isn't fake. It's real. It's the most important thing in my life." His voice was hoarse, but not hoarse enough. Only if he spat out glass would she be satisfied he hurt enough. "God, just give me a chance—"

A tear glinted on his cheek, stark and full. It stopped her dead, until he blinked and she saw his eyes were dry. Ravaged, maybe, but bone dry. That tear belonged to her, an exact match to the dozens swarming her vision.

Are you going to crumple at his feet? Or are you going to stand up and tell him to go to hell?

"Princess, please."

The nickname goaded her into action. Finally. She drew back and stared at him, wanting him to see that she wasn't some broken doll. She'd cracked a little tonight, but the seams would hold. She wasn't going to break, no matter what.

He'd helped her to learn that, and the lesson wasn't one she would forget.

"I'm not your princess. I'm not a fucking princess, period. I'm a fighter, damn you. And I won't give up. For that, I owe you. You gave me the tools to get here, and now I'm going to use them to get you the hell out of my life." She pointed to the door, her finger miraculously steady. "Your tool belt's in the back. Get it on the way out. And unless you plan on seizing this property from me, don't ever fucking come back."

"Alexa." Her name was a sound of pure anguish. She relished it, like a boxer savoring his opponent's wounds.

He lifted a hand toward her and she shrank back, her finger still extended. "I never want to see you again."

For a long moment there was nothing but the sound of the rain pelting the windows and his harsh breaths. Hers had steadied, her heartbeat settling into an even beat. She could fall apart later, after he'd gone.

If he ever left.

"This isn't over," he bit off finally, stalking into the back room. Then he walked past her and out the door, slamming it with a cheery tinkle of bells that signaled the final curtain on what was supposed to be the best night of her life.

Chapter Ten

"You make a piss-poor drunk."

"Yeah, well, you're ugly."

That established, Dillon and Cory bent their elbows at the same time and drank.

Cory slapped down enough money to pay for another round of beer. Shady's Pub might not have much going for it, atmosphere-wise, but the brew was ice-cold. After a few beers and a lot of moping, he even kind of liked the place.

"If it wasn't for you, I wouldn't be here," Dillon mumbled, though he'd already said as much several times before. Easier to keep talking so his misery had no chance to fill his head as it had his heart. If he breathed in too deep, his chest ached. "You caused all of this." Definitely not all, but his drunk brain insisted his brother was to blame for taxes, death, and everything in between.

"Lex's delinquent. Not my fault she hates me. Also not my fault that Met—" Cory stopped, shook his head. "That Melinda isn't interested in me."

"What?" Dillon stared. In the blue-washed light of the bar, Cory looked drunk and morose. And *unkempt*. His hair stuck straight up and his tie hung limply, as if he'd tried to undo it and failed. "You're serious?"

"Yes, well, she'd be perfect to attend events with, but she's dating someone. Then Victoria told me Melinda would never date me because I don't know how to have fun." Cory banged his bottle. "That's crazy. Look at me now. Fun all over."

"Oh yeah." Dillon laughed. Croaked really, but it was something.

When he'd left Divine, he'd been sure he wouldn't laugh again for a very long time. If ever. He'd headed to Cory's office, intent on reading him the riot act for everything he could think of, when his brother had called and asked to meet at Shady's. That was an extremely unusual move for Cory, odd enough Dillon had been compelled to say yes.

It had been a very long time since they'd had a drink together. And they were both pathetically single and obviously destined to remain that way for a while.

"Actually, I'm fun personified." Cory downed more beer. "I signed up to get my chakra read."

"What?"

"Dontcha know what a chakra is?"

"Sounds like New Agey mumbo to me." Dillon uncapped his next brew.

"I even had yogurt and granola for breakfast today. On. A. Whim." Why Cory imparted that with such weighty significance, Dillon had no clue. "Do you know how long I've had Wheaties with skim milk, a glass of OJ, and a cup of black decaf for breakfast? Years, my friend. *Years*."

"I'm not your friend."

"No kidding. Most of the time you won't even speak to me. Now I know why you've been crawling up my ass lately." Cory's charcoal eyes gleamed with unholy amusement. Combined with the sickly cast of his skin from the blue lights, he rather resembled a demented, well-dressed Smurf. "Think I'm gonna let her go scot-free because you wanna bone her?"

Dillon faced front and center, his gaze lasering in on a Rolling Stones poster on the wall. But all he could see were Alexa's stricken eyes.

"You're drunk." Truth be told, they were both soused. Neither drank much as a rule, and clearly they both sought to abandon their mental faculties as fast as humanly possible.

"Am not."

"Are so. You never use the word 'boned.' Normally you call sex 'intercourse.' Never even heard you use slang before. So...drunk."

"Fuck off."

Dillon tipped back his beer. "Why don't you ask out Vick? She'd be way more interesting than Mel."

"I told you, she's too young. Practically a child. She's as fun as a hurricane. Or an ingrown toenail."

Dillon croaked out another semi-laugh. "That's lame."

"No lamer than you being in love with Lex." Cory smiled at him around the mouth of his beer. "She'll never want you because of me. She hates me."

His chest had gone tight in direct contrast to his suddenly spongy brain cells. "Yeah, I gathered that. So I lied like a moron. I *am* a moron."

"No arguments."

He laughed until his jaw throbbed. It was better than banging his head against the bar until he passed out, the only other option on the table. "See why I don't spend more time with you?"

Cory's pause made him glance over in silent question. "You used to like me."

He had, a long time ago. Before sibling rivalry had become the sibling feud from hell. As the years passed, his best friend had turned into his biggest competition—and worse, there was no competing with Cory. He got straight As and had never wavered for a second on his plan for his life. He'd also accepted his role in the business with the zeal of a nerd snapping on his pencil protector. So Dillon had stopped trying to compete, instead choosing to play to his own strengths: enjoying women who enjoyed him right back and rebelling against everything Cory stood for.

Even when what he stood for was exactly what Dillon embraced as well, despite their different approaches.

Working with Alexa—and becoming excited again about marketing and business plans and all the stuff he'd labeled as "pencil pushing" in his mind—had reinvigorated his love of the other side of the desk. He wasn't taking a more active role in the company just because he had to. He *wanted* to.

"I'm back now," Dillon said quietly. "I'm in, one hundred percent."

And this time, he'd make sure they did things right, with a joint focus toward profit and helping smaller businesses thrive whenever possible. He wouldn't skirt the fringes any longer. The only way to ensure that Cory didn't lose sight of the trees in the forest was to keep drilling the branches into his damn brain.

"With the business?" Cory's voice lowered. "Or being my brother?"

Guilt flared on the back of Dillon's tongue, and the beer suddenly tasted sour. "Both. You can count on me."

Cory slanted him a measuring look, then nodded and sipped his drink.

"Since I have lost time to make up for on the brotherly score, you might want to know the 'rents are on the warpath. Since they're gearing up for retirement, once they have more free time their concerns about your lack of a social life are gonna take precedence. Big-time."

"I have a social life," Cory muttered.

Dillon ground the heel of his hand against his suddenly throbbing left eye. Suddenly the place felt like the inside of a toaster oven. "Your right hand doesn't count."

Ignoring him, Cory looked down at the tool belt Dillon had tossed on the stool between them. "What the hell's this?" He withdrew a purple item from one of the pockets and held it up to the light.

Dillon blinked. What looked like tiny butterfly wings extended from the middle of the cylinder, and the rest of the shaft had ridges like a potato chip. He frowned. Or like a—

"Nice vibe." Bobby the bartender smirked as he circled his rag over the bar. "Big plans?"

Cory dropped the vibrator as if he'd learned it was a live nuclear reactor. "That's not mine."

Bobby nodded understandingly. "His?" he asked, jerking his chin at Dillon, who'd snatched up the toy and already put it away. Well, back in his tool belt. His brother touching Alexa's...pleasure tools seemed way wrong. At least he assumed it was hers. Who else's could it be?

"Never leave home without it," Dillon said somberly.

Once Bobby gave them the thumbs-up sign and moved on, Cory leaned closer. "She's plying you with sex toys?"

"She was," he said, unable to elaborate. Even thinking about what had happened at Divine made him want to rip the bar out of the wall. *He'd* done this. Not Cory. His stupid ideas and schemes had landed his ass in this very spot, and damn if it didn't hurt.

More than anything ever had.

"Lucky bastard. By the way, just so you know—the Taste of Froot thing's not happening."

"No?" Dillon couldn't claim to be displeased. Maybe now

Cory would find other kittens to kick than Divine. Though he'd never think of Alexa as a kitten. She was too strong and independent. Too utterly capable of taking care of herself.

And how, judging from the accoutrements he'd just discovered.

"Too bad," Dillon added when Cory didn't respond.

"Victoria's ecstatic. She doesn't want me anywhere near her sister." Cory's scowl deepened. "A fact she's made no effort to hide."

"'Cause she wants to do you herself." Dillon saluted Cory with his beer when he cast sharp eyes in Dillon's direction. "It's plain as fucking day, man."

"You're nuts."

"You never use yours. Otherwise you'd see what's in front of you. She's hot."

One eyebrow poised to leap off Cory's forehead. "*Victoria?*"

"You don't find her even a little attractive?"

The blue spread into a faint purple tinge at Cory's hairline. "Well, of course, she's attractive." His eyes glazed like a sheet of ice. "But hot? No."

Dillon grinned. Yep. Doth man protest way too much, even with doth beer.

"You're having too much sex. It's clouding your judgment."

Not anymore. "Is there such a thing?" Dillon shouted over the sudden uptick in the music.

"Sex? It's been over a year for me." Cory lifted his voice. "*Over a year.*"

The music cut out again just as Cory made his declaration. The words echoed across the bar, as if he'd shouted them. Judging from the ringing in Dillon's ear, he had.

The music shuddered back on with a screech and a pulse

of sound. Dillon shook his head. "'Splains a lot, if you ask me."

"I'm not," Cory snapped, managing to close his mouth as conversations resumed around them. "Asking you."

Dillon shrugged. He had his own problems.

"Are you going to ask her to the benefit?"

Dillon stared into his beer. "I already did," he said finally.

"They're going to give you an award, you know."

"For what?" Dillon snapped.

"You're always busting your ass for that charity. How many houses have you rehabbed this year?"

"A lot. But—"

"But nothing. You deserve the recognition."

"Recognition's the last thing I want right now," Dillon said under his breath.

After tonight's spectacular fail, he didn't give a shit about the benefit. He'd hurt Alexa when all he'd wanted was to help her, so what the hell made him qualified to help anyone else?

He couldn't even take care of the woman he loved. He fucking *loved* her, and he didn't know if he'd ever get a chance to tell her. If she'd ever believe him.

God, he didn't want to lose her.

Cory shifted his way. "It's your business too. If you want to cancel out her debts, no one's stopping you."

The shift in topic made Dillon lift a brow. "She can do it herself." She'd be paying them off soon enough.

"You honestly think she can clear that much back debt? In this economy?" Cory's tone held the evidence of his doubt. "And even if she can, how far behind will that put her for the future? Just maintaining current operating capital will take a toll."

"She can do it," Dillon repeated. "She's already on her way." He slammed down his beer. "She didn't give up on the store, and I'm not fucking giving up on her."

He'd prove to her what he felt. Whatever it took.

• • •

Alexa stewed all night long, tossing and turning on her stupid air mattress. Jeez, she needed a real bed.

Real was the most hateful word in the English language.

Lying alone in the dark, she tried to cry, just to get out some of the pain. But her tears had dried up, spent in the fury she'd unleashed on him at her store. And it still hadn't been enough to close the gaping wound he'd left behind.

She was so in love with the ass. Didn't it just figure that the first time she fell for a guy, it was a lying jerk like Dillon?

But *why* had he lied? That was the one question she just couldn't answer. For sport? To try to take down her business from the inside out? And if so, why had he helped her? There was no denying he had, even if he'd ripped her to the bone afterward.

She finally gave up on trying to sleep and dragged herself through a shower at first light. The moment she entered the kitchen she saw the source of the scratching noises she'd been too worn out to investigate earlier.

Her cat crouched over her prey, looking sickly instead of triumphant, and a fresh wash of tears blurred Alexa's eyes.

The violet was dead.

Oh, technically it probably wasn't. Dirt was scattered over the floor and the leaves looked gnawed on and limp, but if she wanted to replant and nurture it, maybe she could save it from plant heaven. Compared with the dried-out flowers from Dillon she'd foolishly saved that were now lying, crumbled, all over the floor, the violet didn't look half-bad. But she just didn't have the energy. Or the time, since she was late for work.

"You're a bad kitty," Alexa admonished as she scooped the cat into her arms and cuddled her close. What had gotten into her? Trixie was three years old and never got into anything she shouldn't. Or at least she hadn't at the old house. Seemed her cat was having as hard of a time adjusting to their new normal as she was.

She nuzzled Trixie's cheek while she hit the vet's speed dial. Five minutes later she had an emergency vet appointment and her understanding best friend was on the way to Divine to deal with Mrs. Yancy. Thank God for Nellie. She'd have to buy the baby another frilly dress to go with the fifty she'd already stockpiled.

By the time she dropped off her lethargic—but thankfully mostly unharmed—kitty and relieved her best friend at work, her sleepless night had taken its toll in a raging headache. And then it got even worse, because the first thing she saw when she turned on her computer was an e-mail from Santangelo, LLC.

Great. Just great.

She expected to see the record of the funds she'd transferred via phone that morning to pay off her back rent. Instead, there was a note informing her that not only had her payment gone through, she now had a credit balance of approximately three months' rent.

Dillon.

She slammed her fist on the counter. Damn him all to hell. Did he think money would solve everything? If he did, he was no better than his brother.

In all fairness, she'd once believed that, too, but she'd been so wrong. Now that her footing was becoming more solid in the business arena, all she could think about was what she'd been missing. She'd had it for a little while, and by God, she couldn't imagine living her entire life without experiencing that wild rush again.

She wouldn't.

Fingers shaking, she withdrew the ticket Dillon had given her to that evening's gala from her purse. She was a successful store owner. Hiding away in her apartment while she stewed over what he'd done might've fit the old Alexa, who only fought if the odds were firmly stacked in her favor. But the new version wasn't about to give him—and Cory—the satisfaction of thinking she needed to go off to cry in private.

She would be at that party, and she'd be looking so damn good Dillon would be the one weeping by the time the night was through. They'd see that she didn't need their damn help. Or their pity.

• • •

Dillon paced the length of the reception hall. He'd been calling Alexa all day to no avail. He'd gone by the store earlier, but she'd closed at noon, not two as the sign on the door said. Even more worried, he'd pounded on her apartment door. Only after he'd gone back outside had he realized her small sedan wasn't parked in the lot.

He thumbed out a package of antacids from his jeans pocket. He'd been chewing them like mints all day and his gut still burned. His head still throbbed. He was hungover and miserable and God, he couldn't stand the idea of her curled up crying somewhere—or worse. If only she'd let him fix things. He'd make it right.

He'd do anything.

"There you are!" Sidestepping the workers finalizing last-minute arrangements, his mother hurried across the decorated hall. She looked as fresh as one of Alexa's roses in a pale pink shift dress. "I've been trying to reach you all day."

As evidenced by the five voice mails he'd ignored. "Sorry. I've been in the middle of stuff."

"Stuff that didn't include getting changed for tonight, I see." Obviously disappointed, she fingered the sleeve of his T-shirt. "People will start arriving in less than an hour."

He glanced at the tables with their navy tablecloths and drab flower arrangements centered around hurricane lamp-style candles. "Who did the flowers?"

"*We* did the flowers. Have you forgotten the home beautification part of Value Hardware's business?"

He wished he could forget a lot of things. "No, but Divine could've done so much more. Alexa could've..." He stopped. How long was he going to continue to torture himself like this? "I'll go home and get changed soon. It's not like I'm making any headway." Disgust laced his words as he shoved his phone in his pocket.

His mother frowned. "Did you finally find a date for tonight?"

"I'd like to hear the answer to this," a voice behind him answered.

He looked away from his mother. And did a double take at the sight of Alexa in a floor-length royal purple dress, slit up the side to reveal miles of creamy thigh.

His mom looked back and forth between them. "Oh," she said softly.

Dillon stared at Alexa. She stood tall and regal, her hair pulled on top of her head in a crown of curls. Her eyes regarded him coolly. Waiting.

He'd been waiting too. Now was his chance to put it all out there. To say everything he'd felt, to apologize, to tell her how much she meant to him. That the idea of living his life without her in it would be like never seeing the sun again. Everything she'd made so bright and new just from her presence would go dark.

"Yes, *oh*." Alexa flashed a razor-thin smile and cocked her head. "Still wearing the poor-boy costume, huh? Afraid you were going to run into me?"

He barely breathed. *Costume*? He wasn't hiding from her, not in the ways that mattered. She'd helped him figure out who he really was, and how much he could give to the company. Along with how much he would get in return.

It wasn't about coloring outside the lines. It was about working within the system to make it better from the inside out. Helping people through helping himself.

And her. Always her.

"Did you figure paying my bills would make up for your sins?" she demanded.

Dillon gaped at her. "I—"

"I don't need your money, Mr. Big Shot. I can do whatever I need to do for my store myself. It'll succeed or I'll die trying. I didn't want you to help prop up my business. I wanted you for *you*."

His head and stomach churned in tandem. Only half of what she'd said made sense to his addled brain. Why had he chosen last night to get drunk when he needed his faculties more than ever?

All he had left to give her was the truth. He'd get the words out even if they choked him.

And with the way his throat kept locking up, they just might.

"Nothing I did was for show. What you saw is who I am." He ignored her derisive snort. "I wanted to help you, but not because I didn't think you could do it on your own. I knew you could."

"You really think I trust your supposed faith in me when all you've done is lie?" Her beautiful eyes sheened and his gut twisted. "Give me one reason to believe you."

Because I love you.

He opened his mouth, the words right there. This was it. He was going to lay it all on the line. But before he could speak, Alexa muttered a curse and twisted the knife in his gut once more.

"Your money can buy a lot of things, but it can't buy me."

Chapter Eleven

Goddamn bastard.

Alexa flexed her hand and stared straight ahead until her dry eyes screamed for relief. But there was none to be found tonight.

Other women probably would've slapped him and left. She'd planned on doing some version of that but when she'd seen not one, but two different gorgeous women glide up to Dillon before she'd even made it out the door, she'd changed her mind.

She wasn't keeping an eye on him. That would be ridiculous. No, she just wouldn't give him the satisfaction of ducking out early as if she was too brokenhearted to stay.

There were other benefits to staying besides proving that her will hadn't been broken by the mighty Santangelo/James brothers. She wanted to see the so-not-a-handyman in action. Schmoozing with his fellow benefactors, rubbing elbows with his snooty family. Although Dillon's mom and dad weren't snooty at all, truthfully. Cory probably stole all the stuck-up genes and hoarded them for himself. Seemed like something he would do.

It wasn't all bad. She ended up at a table with two lovely older couples who included her in the conversation and seemed quite interested in her store. Both of the women mentioned stopping by the following week. And even a picky eater like her couldn't fault the selection of the dinner buffet. She went for seconds of her chicken piccata, and had a thick wedge of lemon meringue pie for dessert.

Though that might just have been to spite Dillon, who tried repeatedly to speak to her. She hadn't told him to go to hell again, but she reserved the right to change her mind.

The last time he'd crouched next to her table and told her in an urgent voice that she needed to give him a chance, that he'd never meant for "things" to go so far. His face might as well have been set on stun for its effect on her traitorous body.

His golden skin gleamed under the lights and his black tux wrapped sensuously around every rise and ripple of muscle. The few times she'd caught his eye, he'd stared at her as if he wanted nothing more than to get her alone. Worse, her traitorous body wanted to let him. Coming to the benefit at all had not been the smartest move on that score.

She fought a sigh. It just wasn't fair.

The unfairness multiplied when they started the award portion of the evening. Dillon's mother got the first one, then it was two board members' turns. She applauded them all, because it was a great charity and the house she and Dillon had, ahem, visited the other night proved how much good Helping Hands was doing in the community.

How much good *he* was doing.

But when Dillon got the biggest award of all, practically a damn trophy, for all his many hours of service, she couldn't look away fast enough. Even so, she still saw the embarrassment he shouldered as he strode on stage.

He kept his speech mercifully brief. Too brief, it turned

out, since that meant the guests could again wander around. What wandered her way only sent her further into her rage spiral, via emotional purgatory.

"You should've sat at our table. We have beignets."

She narrowed her eyes. "You have a lot of nerve."

"Indeed. It's an asset in business." With a smile unnervingly close to Dillon's—how had she not noticed before?—Cory sat in the empty seat beside her. The dancing portion of the evening had begun, and most of the couples were swarming the dance floor. There weren't too many singles at the gala, and those who were there looked about as merry as she did.

"You look like you just fought three rounds and lost in a TKO."

Wonderful. That was just the image she wanted to project. "I'm fine."

"He said the same thing. He's a worse liar than you."

Something sharp twisted in her already achy chest. "I think he's a pretty good liar, all things considered." She bore down hard on the urge to cry. Just sit there and bawl while the romantic swing music swelled and couples swirled in pastel blurs around them. "I don't need his damn money. I don't need him to bail me out. I paid off my own bills."

Cory rested his leg on his opposite knee, apparently not concerned about his steel-gray tux. The guy might've stepped off a page in *GQ*, he was that handsome. In fact, she might've called him the most gorgeous man in the room, if not for the blond, eye-maskless pirate scowling at the head table. He would win that contest, effortlessly.

In jeans and a T-shirt. In a flawless tux. Or better yet, completely naked.

"You could choose to look at it as a hand, not a handout."

"I can take care of myself," she said, knowing she sounded defensive and stubborn and not giving a hoot. She was entitled.

"Undoubtedly. But I've heard—and this is just a rumor— that life is better when you have someone who wants to take care of you, and vice versa. Someone to spoon with on cold mornings, and bring you soup. Or let out the dog, should you have one."

"I don't have a dog."

"Me either. My parents have a horse, though." Cory seemed to ponder that before shaking his head. "Then there are all those other couples things. Sending cards on important dates. The occasional love note tucked under a pillow. Joint checking accounts."

She barked out a laugh. "Joint checking accounts? That's one of the highlights of romance to you?"

His grin overtook his face and silvered his charcoal eyes. "Trust me, sharing an account with me would be more excitement than most women could take."

"You're a complete ass."

"I am." He leaned toward her, his expression suddenly grave. "But he's not. He's actually a decent guy. Part of why women are constantly flinging their undergarments in his direction, despite his assertions that they only care about his wallet. He's the kind of man women can sniff from miles away."

She'd already seen several of those types skulking around him tonight. Not that she blamed them. But still. "I'm assuming you're referring to the stink from his lies."

"I guarantee he hated himself for lying to you." At her huff of breath, Cory zoomed in for the kill. "He's faithful and genuine and loyal. Above all that, no matter what you think, he's honest. He didn't lie to hurt you. I promise you that. Dill's not built that way. Me, on the other hand, I'm apt to do any damn thing. For any damn reason."

Shocker. "I thought I knew him. At least part of him. But I don't. He's a complete mystery."

"Because you didn't know I was his brother? Until recently, he hasn't acted as if I am for years."

She didn't know what to say to that. Worse, she wasn't sure if she hurt more for herself or for Dillon at that moment, if Cory was telling the truth. "You can tell him I don't need his money. I want that credit on my account returned."

"How about mine?"

Alexa glared at him. "What's that supposed to mean?"

"He didn't pay your bill. He doesn't even know it *has* been paid."

"Then who—" She broke off when Cory shot to his feet, as quick as a rattlesnake. "Oh, *hell* no."

"We've had an excellent quarter." He dipped his hands into his pockets, a mercurial smile flitting over his face. "It was either pay off your back bill or expand the store's gardening section. Your choice."

Before she could rail at him, he strolled away. Whistling.

The bastard. That family seemed to make them in pairs.

To avoid further bloodshed, she remained seated through the dancing portion of the gala. Luckily one of the wives returned sans husband to keep her company. They people-watched for over an hour. The nicest part was that Ruth never asked her if she was dating anyone. It helped her pretend she was single and unencumbered.

The single bit was true at least.

Eventually the auction got under way. She watched as a parade of high-end electronics and vacation packages to various tropical islands got offered up for bid. Everything went for staggeringly high amounts. Then the last item was put up, a simple watercolor painting of a purple rose, its petals so velvety and lush she would've sworn the flower was real.

The simple wooden frame surrounded what looked like a burlap canvas.

Under the table, she gripped her hands together.

"This one is called *Love at First Sight*," the emcee read from his card. "Gorgeous, isn't it? So, who's going to start the bidding?" he asked in his booming voice, his smile bright enough to scare the sun.

The irony of that particular rose being featured in this particular auction wasn't lost on her, but she refused to look Dillon's way to see if he was staring.

Watercolors. Not often anymore. Don't have the time.

Had he really done this painting for her? And what did it mean exactly, other than it being the rose he knew she loved the most?

She rubbed her forehead. Cripes, she was going to have an aneurysm if she didn't stop with the questions.

"Three hundred?" She glanced at Ruth as she bid three-fifty, and a sudden panic seized her. That was *her* painting. If someone had snatched it up at a flea market and slapped a hefty price tag on it, the joke would be on her but she didn't care.

Alexa lifted her paddle. "Four hundred," she called, shocked she sounded so calm. Her heart sped up while she waited for the auctioneer to acknowledge her winning bid, but before he could, another bid came from the table in front she'd steadfastly avoided looking at all night.

"Five hundred." Dillon's even tone made her sit up straighter. Why had he done the painting for her if he just wanted to snatch it back? Had their fight made him rescind the gesture? Or change his mind?

Whatever. She was getting that painting. It was hers, and suddenly it seemed vital she win it.

"Six," she called back.

"Seven," Dillon immediately countered, earning a growl from her that made her tablemates glance at her in dismay.

Fine, if he wanted to play that way, she was game. So what if he took baths in beaucoup bucks. She had credit cards. Okay, she had one credit card left. With a low limit. "Nine," she yelled, louder than was necessary.

Out of the corner of her eye, she noticed Dillon's parents looking in her direction. And Cory, that jerk, was grinning.

"Two thousand," Dillon shot back.

She tossed her purse on the table. Oh hell no. She was going to hang the painting above the prep table in her store and he was not taking it from her. With all the embarrassment and frustration—and yes, pain—Dillon had caused her, she wasn't letting go that easily.

One thing he'd taught her—if nothing else—was to fight.

"Five thousand." She slapped down her paddle when a wave of conversation rolled through the crowd.

"Ten thousand," Dillon returned, rising.

Slowly he crossed the room and it took everything inside her not to wilt against her chair. He'd loosened his bow tie, shrugged off the jacket. With his strong jaw, his sexy glower, and the stubbled growth of beard, she was practically toast. Add in his untucked white dress shirt open at the neck to reveal his sun-warmed skin—skin she'd kissed and licked and bitten—and yeah, she was *so* done for.

The last of the fight drained out of her. She'd battled her ass off for that painting, for her store, because he'd been there. Pushing her. Showing her everything she could have if she didn't give up.

God, he'd *wanted* her to fight all along.

When she descended back to reality and realized he was at her side, she opened her mouth. She intended to tell him to go to hell. What came out was a soft, croaked, "Why?" As if she were on the verge of tears.

Worse, as if they were already tracking down her cheeks. Again.

Now he would know how much she cared, if he didn't already.

"Can we call the bidding at ten thousand?" the auctioneer asked, waiting for Alexa's argument.

She gave none. She'd lost anyway, hadn't she? The guy had more money than God apparently, so why waste everyone's time on pissing matches?

"Sold to Mr. James for ten thousand dollars. The charity appreciates your generous donation—twice over in this case."

"Princess?"

She braced at the nickname. Soft fingertips skimmed her jaw and she glanced up, hating that she was still crying. Two crying jags a year were usually her limit, and she'd hit more than that within the past twenty-four hours. Not good.

Before she could speak—though she had no clue what to say—he crouched at her side, his fingers exerting a tender pressure as he turned her face to his. "You asked me why. Let me explain. No more lies. Just the truth."

"What is there to—"

She jolted as he fisted his hands in her hair, wrecking her careful updo, and dragged her toward him, nearly upending her chair in the process. Her gasp at the pull of gravity that slammed her into his chest turned into a moan when he swept his tongue between her lips and simply took what she'd been trying so hard to lock away.

The familiarity almost broke her. His touch, his smell, the way his nose bumped hers in his urgency to seize her mouth. He took possession of her with confidence, the kind she'd found so sexy once upon a time. If she'd only tasted his skill in the kiss, she would've shoved him back and told him to go to hell. But she could sense the desperation in each conquering stroke of his tongue and every strangled groan trapped in his throat.

His teeth scraped her lower lip as he drew back, his eyes steady on hers. Wildly blue and hot with need, those eyes made her want to believe. "I love you, Alexa. *You* were the only thing worth risking you for. If taking back what I did means I couldn't be there to watch you succeed, I wouldn't do it."

Her head pounded, making his words rattle around like pinballs. She simply couldn't process what he'd said, not after he'd already shaken her down to her toes with that scorcher of a kiss. Her lips were still tingling. *Everything* was still tingling.

The sound of clapping made her glance around the banquet hall. Everyone seemed to be grinning at her and Dillon. She, the woman who was so aware of how she was behaving at all times, hadn't even noticed that they'd created a spectacle.

"Don't look at them. Look at me."

His demand might've rankled, had she not been breathing hard and close to seeing spots. The heavy weight of everyone's gazes burned her skin, as if every guest had a personal stake in her reply. It was all too much. "You stole my painting," she blurted out.

"No, I didn't," he said, his voice low. Rough. "I painted it for you. It's yours."

"You misrepresented yourself to me. You're one of *them*."

His grimace helped mitigate the sting in her eyes. A little. But a woman in a teal pantsuit walked over before he could respond, a brown-paper-wrapped package in her hands. "Here you go, Dill. Thanks." She cast a quick glance at Alexa. "Lucky lady," she said with a smile before walking away.

He set the package in her lap as the auction resumed

behind them. "They aren't so bad, I swear. My stepfather likes that you don't back down." His warm breath against her ear elicited a shiver she was powerless to stop. "He's impressed by how you marched in here and gave me hell. Said I deserved it and more for what I did."

It would be so easy—too easy—to let herself be swept along by that kiss and how much she already missed him. His grand gesture and attentive expression didn't hurt, either. It was as if he really cared, as if he hadn't just played her because he could.

As if he loved her.

"Come with me," he said, dragging his thumb over her lip. Then he added that magical word. "Please."

His nearness had a disturbing way of making her want to lean into him, to let him caress her hair and take care of her as he had so many times already. "Where?"

He rose and extended his hand only long enough to help her up. The hope in his eyes, the soft vulnerability of it, prompted her to stand as well. "I have something to show you."

She followed him outside to the parking lot, her throat oddly tight. She'd grown used to him grabbing her hand when they walked together. For him not to felt weird. And awful. "Can you just leave? It's your benefit. They gave you a fancy award."

"We're leaving. I'll make my apologies later." He gestured to his bike, hulking in the darkness. "Are you okay to ride in that?"

She looked at her gown. The appropriate answer was "hell no" but she didn't want to be appropriate tonight. She was too pissed off, too raw, too desperate for him to have any sort of explanation that made sense. "Yeah." She held the picture under one arm and hiked up her dress. "I can do it."

"Christ, you're hot," he muttered, sounding somewhat dismayed by the fact. Then he marched over to his bike and held out his spare helmet. Before she tried to fumble it on, he set it on her head and did the strap up himself. Which was when she realized that *shit*, she was actually going to have to ride his bike.

Wind. Fast speeds. Certain death. Did she really feel like playing the odds tonight?

"We could take my car instead."

He frowned. "You *are* worried about the dress."

"I'm worried about *me*." She tossed a glance at his bike. "That thing's huge."

Lots of other guys would've winked and made some sort of joke. Dillon only nodded. "I'll keep you safe. I promise." He tipped up her chin and stared down at her, his features silvered in the moonlight. "You're important to me, Alexa. I know you don't believe that yet, but I hope you will eventually."

She didn't reply, just followed his instructions to get on behind him. Her arms locked around his muscular torso and she pressed close when he kicked the bike into gear, both out of sheer terror and to protect her painting. She would've shelled out five grand for it, she'd be damned if it got crushed or broken.

Not that she cared about the painter. Or the reason he'd chosen that subject. Not at all.

Wind whipped through her hair as the bike leaned and lurched through the ride. After a couple minutes, she finally stopped clutching his abdomen quite so tightly and pried open her eyes. It was such a gorgeous night, hot and breezy, with the scent of impending fall in the air. And she was holding on to a sexy-as-hell guy who made her feel safe, just as he'd sworn he would.

She wished they weren't fighting so she could just savor

every moment of this. Dillon and the night and the bike rumbling between her thighs.

Too soon, they were pulling up outside her building. He stopped the bike and took off his helmet before looking back at her, a smile playing around his mouth. "You laughed."

A bit dazed, she removed her own helmet. Once he'd gotten off, he lifted her to the ground, something she might've balked at had her legs not been the consistency of gummy candy. "Did I? It was probably from terror."

"Even so. It only lasted a second but I heard it. I love it when you laugh." He brushed her hair out of her face and took her helmet, setting both aside before grabbing her hand. The rightness of the gesture registered first, drowning out her complaints.

He'd lied and misled her. And right now, he looked down at her as if he was counting the stars reflected in her eyes.

"Come on," he murmured, leading her around the back of the building. Once inside, he tugged her up the stairs.

"Where are we going?" she asked, though she knew the moment they passed her floor.

Where it had all begun for them.

They emerged on the roof, and the questions in her throat turned into a sigh. The entire area was ringed in white lights, and between the small spotlights were purple roses, their velvety petals illuminated in the darkness. With green plants blanketing every available surface except the pathway she and Dillon stood on, she felt as if she'd stepped into a walled jungle covered by a canopy of moonlight.

Her attention landed on the solar panels she must've missed before and everything he'd said to her last night clicked into place. "This is yours. You not only came up with the concept, it's your building."

He slipped his hands in his pockets and managed to look

simultaneously stoic and sheepish. "Technically my parents own it."

"You really believe in this stuff," she said, releasing her hair from its clip. Her head still ached, but it was getting better. "Green roofs, and doing better for the environment. It's not just about saving cash."

"No."

"And you designed all this. This gorgeous area, it's all you?"

"I don't know that it's gorgeous, but yeah. All me. Who would I ask for help? Cory'd laugh at me if I showed him this. He'd tell me to stop screwing with flowers and do some real work."

It wasn't even what he said so much as the way he said it, with his jaw tight and his gaze on the skyline. As if he had no clue of the functional beauty he'd created.

"I like it when you screw with flowers," she said quietly. She tucked the small painting under her arm and stepped closer to lay a hand on his chest.

He glanced at her, his wariness evident in every line of his face. "You could do so much more with this than I ever could. I was serious about the houses. If you'd be willing to lend some of your expertise, we could make them even better for the people who move in. Both environmentally and—Christ, what's the word I want?"

"Artistically?" she guessed.

"Yeah." He heaved out a breath. "When you get so close to me, it's like all the wires cross in my head."

"Only there?"

"No. *Fuck* no." His grimace proved just how true that was. "But I can't start talking about my dick when you already think I am one."

She didn't laugh, but she wanted to. Instead she tilted her

head and removed her hand. It was far too easy to touch him, and they had to talk. "Why didn't you tell me who you really are?"

"I did," he said, hissing out a breath when she rolled her eyes. "Okay, I didn't tell you the whole story. I should've said Cory was my brother. Who my parents were. It had never even occurred to me to hide it until you thought I was the handyman. Then I couldn't help going along, to see what would happen. I'm used to women wanting me for my money, so you not thinking I had any and still flirting with me was a novelty."

"The panty flingers," she said under her breath.

His brows knitted. "Huh?"

"Go on."

He eyed her, but continued. "I liked that you were seeing *me*, not my connection to Value Hardware. Even so, I wouldn't have kept the lie going beyond that afternoon in the bathroom, when you were hostile about the store." He blew out a breath. "Then there was the roof, and after that you started ranting about Value Hardware—"

"I did not rant."

"What would you call it?"

Ranting. "Expressing a strong, well-validated opinion."

One side of his mouth lifted. "Fine. But your well-validated opinion made me shut my mouth, because I, well…"

"What?" she demanded.

"I wanted you." He stared out into the darkness. She didn't know if he was studying the high-rises or the dark hills—or even the star-studded sky—but from the clench of his fist at his side, he wasn't moved by the scenery. "I wasn't trying to save the world or even your business. I barely even knew Divine Flowers existed. But I knew you had the prettiest, saddest blue eyes I'd ever seen."

She turned her head and there was the daisy watering can. The memories it brought back made her smile—and want to cry.

"I tried to tell you that first night on the roof. Not hard," he admitted. "But I tried. Then you kissed me, and you could've threatened me with water torture and I wouldn't have done a thing to end it. I'm not proud of that, but it's the sterling truth. I would've said I could shoot rainbows out of my ass to keep your mouth on mine."

She could feel herself weakening, turning to Alexa-shaped mush. If he was just spouting lines, she had to give him credit. "And after that?"

"I fell in love with your business. As soon as I walked in your store, I saw the possibilities. And I saw how happy it made you. I wanted you to succeed. Dammit, I wanted to help you, and I knew you'd never hear me out if you knew I was Cory's brother. It was selfish, and it was stupid, but I told myself that the end result was more important than ethics. Which is bullshit."

"Not entirely," she said when he walked over to the concrete railing. But he didn't seem to hear her, and she couldn't speak over the ball that formed in her throat at the sight of him outlined in white light.

"I never meant to hurt you. I wish that I hadn't. But I can't take it back, and honestly, as bad as it feels to know you probably hate me, I wouldn't go back. Yeah, it was fun pretending to be someone else for a while. Someone with fewer responsibilities, who could fish or paint or whatever the hell he wanted with his free time."

She stared at him. Did he really think that was the image he'd projected? "You were busy every minute. Working at the apartments. Working at the donor house. You even worked your ass off for *me*."

And that was the bottom line, wasn't it? He hadn't had to do any of the things he'd done for her. Helping her with the arrangements, sharing his ideas—in a rather overbearing manner, granted—and offering his support. None of that had been faked. She would never believe it.

Whatever else he'd done, he truly cared. About her. About Divine. Her heart skipped. Maybe he really did lo—

"My parents are retiring, Alexa. That means I'm going to be consumed with Value Hardware and the income properties from now on, along with the charity." His look radiated through her right down to the soles of her feet. "And you know what? I'm glad my parents can retire, knowing their sons are in control. We've fucking got it, and we're not going to run the damn business they spent their lives building into the ground. I love you, but I can't deny who I am, for you or anyone. As much as I wished I could for a while, if that meant you'd stay in my life, I can't. I'm sorry." His chest rose and fell as if he was sucking in a deep breath. "God, I'm so fucking sorry."

She walked over to him and stood at the high rail, staring down at the slumbering city below. The clutch of yellow balloons on Value Hardware's sandwich board sign waved in the breeze, barely distinguishable at this distance. But she recognized them.

"That smiley face makes me want to punch something," she said in a low voice.

"I know." He chuckled. "Cory, too. Now that we're moving into more of the lifestyle end, he bitches constantly about how he's supposed to launch a high-end magazine when Value's logo is a damn smiley face."

"High-end, hmm?"

"Yes. He's working with Vicky Townsend on it. Well, if they don't kill each other. But now that my mom's stepping down, we're going to need to hire consultants on the gardening end of things." He stroked her hair, just one slow sweep down the length of it. "You'd be perfect for the job."

• • •

As if she'd say yes.

Please say yes.

Alexa slanted him a look. "Me, work with Cory?"

At least she hadn't discounted it out of hand. When she'd refused to acknowledge his declaration of love, he'd thought his entire plan was doomed to fail. "You could work with me more than him. It's his brainchild, but we're working together. Happy fucking family and all that." Dillon cleared his throat. "Assuming working with me would be any better."

"I'm still figuring that out." She stepped closer and placed her hands on his stomach. He shuddered at just that simple contact. "I'll be pretty busy with the store. Especially since I still need to hire a designer. Nellie will be going out on maternity leave in a couple months, and if business keeps up—"

"It will," he interjected, unable to keep his hands out of her hair. The dark wavy mass spilled over his fingers like finely spun silk. "You're going to do amazing."

"You probably won't have much time to help me anymore."

"If you can even call what I did help, then yeah, I'll help. I'll make the time."

She angled her head, her glossy mouth soft and wet. He started to lean in before he caught himself, then shuddered again. Such temptation she presented without even knowing it. "Aren't I your competition?"

"No." He linked an arm around her waist. "We're on the

same side. We can help each other and both businesses will thrive. We'll figure out boundaries, delineate what which store does best. And we won't step on each other's toes." He glided his fingers down her cheek. "Just give me a chance, princess."

A tremor went through her, as fast as lightning. "I'd like to work with you."

Joy swamped him, though he knew it was only the first step. But still, they were moving forward again. "You won't regret it." He cupped her chin in tense fingers. "I promise."

She stared into his eyes, her vulnerability as plain as the white light shimmering on her skin. Knowing how much she despised opening herself up to those feelings, to him, only made them more precious. "I could never regret you," she whispered.

"I'm going to kiss you. Hell, I *have* to kiss you." He brushed his lips over hers and tasted the lemon from her dessert. Then, diving deeper, tasted her, the hot, sultry flavor that made his groin ache and his throat close around a plea for more.

"Dillon James." She breathed his name on a sigh that made him stone-hard. "That's who you are."

"Yes." Locking his arms around her waist, he hauled her up into his arms, kissing her with all the weeks of pent-up frustration and worry. He dragged a hand down to cup her ass, holding her close while she laughed through their kiss and kept hold of her painting.

"I want who you are. Just the way you are, and how you fit with me," she added against his lips.

He clutched her that much closer and nipped the pulse under her jaw, breathing in her freesia scent as if it were more vital than air. Right then, it was. "I want you too. And I want to be by your side when your store kicks so much ass, you can pay Cory back with interest."

Her lips curved. "You say the sweetest things."

"I have so much faith in you, princess. All I want is the chance to earn yours again."

"It wasn't all your fault." She hunched her shoulders. "It was pretty obvious I wasn't rational about Value Hardware, so no wonder you didn't want to tell me. Not letting you off the hook, but just saying I get why you didn't rush to get it out there." She licked her lips and all the blood drained into his cock, which luckily she did not know. He doubted she'd find it endearing while she was being so earnest. "You helped me so much, in so many ways. With the store, by being a friend. By being more. For the first time since Jake and Nellie hooked up and skipped off to Happyville, I didn't feel so alone."

"You want that too?" He tried to keep his tone easy. "What they have?"

"Yeah. I think I do. It's better than I thought it ever would be. Feeling like this," she murmured.

He couldn't hold back another second. Even if she shot him down again. Third time's the charm, right? "I meant what I said, Alexa. I love you."

Her eyes went wide as water spattered them. "Ah, there's our rain. Must be a good sign." She smiled as if she hadn't heard him at all.

"Uh, baby…" he began, trying to shove his jagged emotions back in line.

When the water turned off, then popped back on as the sprinklers swept the plants, she laughed and cupped his jaw. "You're even making it rain for me now."

Returning her grin, he pressed his wet forehead to hers. "I'd do anything for you. Anything."

"Including refusing to be anyone but who you are. That's exactly who I want." Her eyes brightened, a beacon in the darkness. "And who I love."

Emotion moved through him, warm and sweet. Yes, it had been worth going through what they had if it meant they'd end up right here.

He cleared his throat. "I just remembered I still have something that belongs to you. It's purple and ribbed and has several speeds. Low, medium, and call the cops."

Alexa threw back her head and laughed. "Have you been playing with my toys, Mr. James?"

He pulled her toward the door. "Not yet, but if you think you can clear your schedule this evening…"

She pinched his hip. "Schedule? What schedule? I'm all yours."

Dillon grinned. Those were the best three words he'd ever heard.

Well, second best.

Acknowledgments

To my fantabulous editor, Heather Howland, for her patience and mad editing skills!

And to Gina L. Maxwell, whose excitement to read this book made me even more excited to write it.

About the Author

USA TODAY bestselling author Cari Quinn saves the world one Photoshop file at a time in her job as a graphic designer. At night, she writes sexy romance, drinks a lot of coffee, and plays her music way too loud. When she's not scribbling furiously, she's watching men's college basketball, reading excellent books, and causing trouble. Sometimes simultaneously.

www.cariquinn.com

Unleash your inner vixen with these sexy bestselling Brazen releases...

Wrong Bed, Right Guy by **Katee Robert**

Prim and proper art gallery coordinator Elle Walser is no good at seducing men. She slips into her boss's bed in the hopes of winning his heart, but instead, finds herself in the arms of Gabe Schultz, his bad boy nightclub mogul brother. Has Elle's botched seduction led her to the right bed after all?

Seducing Cinderella by **Gina L. Maxwell**

Mixed martial arts fighter Reid Andrews needs to reclaim his title. Lucie Miller needs seduction lessons to catch the eye of another man. They agree to help each other, but by the end of their respective trainings, Reid and Lucy might just discover they've already found what they desire most...

Down for the Count by **Christine Bell**

After Lacey Garrity's wedding day goes horribly, adulterously wrong, she shucks her straight-laced life and accepts a reckless challenge from sexy boxer Galen Thomas, her best friend's older brother. The dare? Take him on her honeymoon instead, but will running away with the enemy lead Lacey to love?

Her Forbidden Hero by **Laura Kaye**

Former Army Special Forces Sgt. Marco Vieri has never thought of Alyssa Scott as more than his best friend's little sister, but her return home changes that. Now that she's back in his life, will he become her forbidden hero, and can she heal him, one touch at a time?

One Night with a Hero **by Laura Kaye**
After growing up with an abusive, alcoholic father, Army Special Forces Sgt. Brady Scott vowed never to have a family of his own. But when a hot one-night stand with new neighbor Joss Daniels leads to an unexpected pregnancy, can he let go of his past and create a new future with her?

Tempting the Best Man **by J. Lynn**
Madison Daniels has worshipped her brother's best friend since they were kids, but they've blurred the lines before and now they can't stop bickering. Forced together for her brother's wedding getaway, will they call a truce or strangle each other first?

Tempting the Player **by J. Lynn**
After the paparazzi catches him in a compromising position, baseball bad boy Chad Gamble is issued an ultimatum: fake falling in love with the feisty redhead in the pictures, or kiss his multi-million dollar contract goodbye. Too bad being blackmailed into a relationship with Chad is the last thing Bridget Rodgers needs.

Recipe for Satisfaction **by Gina Gordon**
Famous bad boy restaurateur Jack Vaughn is trying to find his way back to the living when he meets the beautiful Sterling Andrews, a professional organizer hell-bent on seducing the tattooed hottie as part of her fresh take on life. Too bad she's Jack's newest employee, and totally off-limits.